REFLECTION

REFLECTION

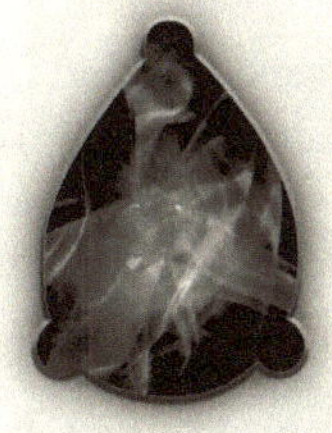

CRYSTAL NICOLE

First edition
ISBN (paperback): 979-8990984202
ISBN (hardcover): 979-8990984219
ISBN (ebook): 979-8990984226

Front cover design by Celin Graphics and Benita Thompson
Cover wraps by Benita Thompson
Chapter illustration by Kaori Keiroz
Typesetting by Benita Thompson

TABLE OF CONTENTS

PROLOGUE

THE QUAINT VILLAGE OF IVOR HAD JUST SETTLED FOR THE NIGHT. Markets were closed and fireplaces lit before the townsfolk snuggled into their beds. Winter would end soon, but little did they know that the season ahead would be dark.

A cold blue light seeped into view outside the boundaries of the village. The flickering light turned purple and black as a set of hands pulled it apart until an oval-shaped portal opened. The creature that stepped into the world of Elohi appeared to be a man, except his skin was calloused and blackened—he was an avro. Claws dangling by his sides, he fluttered his bat-like wings and let out a menacing screech. More of his kind flooded out of the portal behind him.

Amid the monstrous beings stood one creature larger than the rest. With his right hand gripping a red, glowing stone, he strode through the village. Each footstep caused the ground beneath him to quake, waking the villagers.

It started with one tall, blonde, scrawny man, who made eye contact with the creature. His eyes glistened in awe at the terrifying beast and a desire overcame him. His mind became opened in a way it never had before. He wanted that strength, that power...

As evil filled his heart, the man began to turn. His heart thumped as his skin was seared by the darkness. Sharp black nails formed outward from his hands and ragged wings protruded out of his back. Though he was an avro now—his eyes purple—his yellow hair and thin body remained.

Soon after, the avros infiltrated the minds of nearly every human in the community, filling them with a heavy brokenness. In a matter of minutes, avros turned many people of Ivor into monsters.

Up until that moment, Elohi had been a place without monsters or magic, but on that horrific winter night, entered the world.

The air grew still for a moment, as those who were able to withstand the darkness—leaving them unturned—peeked through their windows with shaky breaths. The people who had been turned deserted their homes, following the one with the fiery stone. A sinister gloom hovered over Elohi

Shortly afterward, an army of wolves entered Elohi through the portal—Sairens. They resembled normal wolves, but were twice the size and had feathered wings. They were also able to take human form.

Racing after Arah, the Sairens ran into a massive army of avros who'd formerly been human. The Sairens were forced to abandon their chase to fight the avros.

The Sairens were ill-equipped on their own to take down Arah and his growing numbers that were spreading all over Elohi. So, the Sairens split up into packs, each residing in a single region that they vowed to protect—keeping evil under control.

The avro leader sat on his throne with a staff containing a crimson stone held tightly in his grasp. One of his subjects approached.

"Lord Arah."

"Yes?" Slumped in his seat, Arah twirled the magic rod.

"T-there has b-been a, um—" the timid creature stuttered, but the avro leader cut him off.

"Spit…it…out," Arah demanded through clenched teeth, tightening his grip on the staff. Arah was three times the size of the avro in front of him and known to be quick-tempered.

"Right." The avro cleared his throat. "There has been a sort of p-proclaimed prophecy on the rise, s-sire." He stumbled backwards as Arah swiftly rose to his feet.

"Prophecy?" he yelled, creating an echo down the castle halls. Once his voice stopped bouncing off the walls, Arah's head snapped back around to stare at his messenger. "What sort of prophecy?"

With a sharp inhale, the avro continued. "The Sairen wolves…they speak of o-one they call the R-red Wolf."

Arah's eyes narrowed at his subject, tilting his head side to side as if he was trying to figure something out. The avro leader returned to his throne, snorting. To the smaller avro's surprise, Arah let out a small snicker that quickly became an all-out cackle.

"Right, right…" Wiping tears from his eyes, he calmed himself down. "You mean the Sairen wolf *king?*" Arah leaned forward. "*Red Wolf,*" he mocked. "The Sairens have been dreaming of the day their precious king would be born of the Light and grow to save the world. Was it three red crescent moons he'd show to have on his forehead? Absolute nonsense."

"M-my lord. There is an interesting detail about the d-dream you may want to hear."

Ignoring him, Arah rambled on. "Besides, wasn't he suppose to be born in that other useless world, Yara? Oh, that's right…he'd be stuck there anyway since I sealed the portal."

Fidgeting with his fingers, the avro dropped his head, but didn't give up. "You'll w-want to hear this, my lord."

Arah pulled himself upright and his breath hitched. "Out with it, then."

Swallowing hard, the avro held back a wince and continued. "The people of Elohi s-seem to have f-found a new hope, sire. B-because of a vision about one born under a blood moon…a Sairen wolf specifically."

Giving a blank stare, Arah propped his chin against his fist. "Alright, then," he said nonchalantly. "Just take care of any Sairen wolf born during a blood moon. Wipe them all out." He grinned, waving off the avro, who skittered away to do his bidding.

Left alone now, the avro leader spun his staff in his hand, watching as the mighty stone pulsed and glowed. A swirl of black had invaded its radiance.

"Patience," he whispered to the powerful rock. "In due time, all will bow to me…including you.

THE BLOODCURDLING SCREAM ECHOED THROUGHOUT THE FOREST. Panic bloomed inside me. A way behind me, the entire pack sprinted through the woods. My eyes were fixed on the massive redwoods ahead. Somewhere among them, an avro was taking over a human's heart and filling it with darkness. Even if we were too late to save the young boy, I wanted that horrible, twisted being dead.

I listened closely and waited for the wind to carry the avro's scent in my direction. Beneath the sound of running paws, I heard the creature's feet stumbling around, snapping a flimsy branch lying on the ground. Just as the breeze picked up, my nose began to burn with the stench of human blood.

Not today.

"Come on, Lorraine. You've got this," I told myself.

My feet sprang forward in a sprint. Us Sairen wolves did not typically fly, because it made us easy to spot and wore us out twice as fast as running at full speed. Distantly, I could hear the rest of the pack trailing behind me. Huffs and puffs filled the air from the runt, Luke. I shook my head, still racing to save the small human boy. It wasn't my fault my pack couldn't keep up.

There's no time to lose.

I slowed as I spotted the evil creature through the trees. His bat-like wings drooped on each side, useless, since avros couldn't fly. His skin resembled that of a large reptile. The smug grin lighting the dark-violet rims of his eyes told me the boy standing before him had fully given in to the darkness. Pausing, I watched carefully as his grin widened. The avro was using his power to manipulate the child's emotions and take control.

A violent shiver ran down my spine as I watched the avro's fingers repeatedly curl and open, a black glow emanating from them. The boy's face turned void as he just stood there in front of the monster. Anger pulsed through me. I ran toward the avro, ready to attack, but was stopped dead in my tracks by the ringing voice of the temporary leader of our pack, Cylus Callan.

"Don't. Move."

I glared at Cylus as he materialized behind me with the rest of the pack, minus Luke. They had all transformed into humans, black uniforms intact, and were collectively attempting to catch their breath. The full moon highlighted Cylus's smooth, dark skin. His menacing silver eyes darted between the avro and myself. With just a flick of his wrist, Cylus was on all fours in his Sairen wolf form. His muscles tensed; the black guard hairs that lined his grey fur stood on end. His lip curled as he released a vicious snarl.

The magic of the Light that changed us within seconds, keeping clothes or fur intact, suddenly transformed the rest of the pack into Sairen wolves: canine-shaped creatures with feathered wings, much bigger than the average wolf.

We surrounded our enemy, holding our position as the

young human boy started babbling incoherently. He began to pace, dragging his feet in front of the avro. We all remained still, anxious for the avro's next move.

"What? Did I do something wrong?" the disgusting creature asked sarcastically. He lifted his bloodied claw and scratched his chin. "We were just having some fun."

We?

An uncontrollable rumble began in my chest. The corner of my upper lip rose, exposing my teeth. I could smell more avros closing in on our circle. The atmosphere grew tense as the other monsters came from a distance, while the one we surrounded mind-controlled the small boy to pause and guard him.

I looked to my right and noticed Shariee standing apart from Cylus and myself. Her angel-like wings fluttered anxiously until her younger brother finally caught up to us. The avro swiftly turned his head to look at Luke as the runt joined us in cornering him.

Everyone remained in position; not a soul dared to move. I glared at the avro. I had suddenly noticed the all-too-familiar tear on the avro's left wing. My blood began to boil.

As if Cylus could hear my thoughts, he barked, "Keep your cool, Lorraine, or so help me, I'll—"

My muscles tightened as I leaped into the air.

"Lorraine, please!" Shariee hollered from behind me.

I was already in motion. I angled downward, pursuing my attack. Regret stabbed me as the small boy fell to the ground just before I sank my teeth into the ugly creature's shoulder. The boy had been pierced in the abdomen by the claws of the monster who had taken control of his mind.

I yanked the avro to the ground with my teeth. My heart pounded as the other avros closed in on us. Chaos had unfolded in an instant.

"Oh, no." Shariee grew frantic as she ran to the small boy,

using her magic to change back to human form. She shook him, on the verge of tears. "Please wake up," she cried.

"Uh, sis," Luke said out loud in his wolf form. He twisted his head back as he stood guard over his older sister. Wide-eyed and panting, he froze.

"He's gone, Shariee. Get up," Cylus growled, hurdling over her to face the incoming avros. My nerves twisted into knots as Luke took a few steps back. I could see it in his eyes, the way they frantically bounced back and forth. He was afraid. The runt had only turned fifteen five months ago, the age a Sairen wolf is deemed a warrior and invited to fight alongside the pack.

A lump formed in my throat as I watched Luke come face-to-face with our enemy. I let go of the avro, who winced.

"Shariee!" Luke repeated through gritted teeth as another avro approached the siblings.

I took a step towards them, but when I heard the original avro trying to get up, I stopped and whirled. He gripped his shoulder and grunted in pain. Red-hot rage infiltrated my core.

My wings jerked back. Before I knew it, I was standing on top of the creature, my snout mere inches from his face. The sounds of my pack fighting the newly arrived avros faded into the background.

"Where is he?" I snarled. Pressing my paw against his throat only seemed to amuse him. A fiery pulse pumped through my veins.

"Ah, I remember you," he chuckled.

I glared at him. "If death is that funny to you, I'll have you rolling on the floor."

"Heh. You know what's funny, Snowball?" He nodded at my white fur, his eyes taunting me. I applied more weight to his neck. He whispered hoarsely, "Your brother wasn't as much fun."

I lunged at him. My jaw opened and my teeth sank into his

throat. As life fled from his eyes, I lifted my head to see our quest had failed. Several avros lay dead on the ground, while the rest had fled. I glanced around at everyone's faces, noticing that at some point Alden, an elderly Sairen wolf, had stepped in. He hobbled forward on his cane.

Grief filled my heart as his face sagged with disappointment. Alden's mix of grey and white hair appeared silver in the moonlight. Though he still had the strength to fight as a Sairen wolf, his legs stumbled in his human form. He appeared calm, but his words sent a pulse through my entire body, making me tremble.

"Lorraine. You killed our only lead. How can we find your brother now?"

JUST OUTSIDE OF THE VILLAGE OF HYRA—THE ONLY COMMUNITY of humans remaining in the Terah Region—was Alden's cabin, a place the pack temporarily called home. Everyone was quiet and subdued tonight as they lounged around in the main living space of the cabin. Even the lake just outside was silent and still. We were all in our human forms, as we liked to be when not fighting or searching for avros.

I paced back and forth, my thoughts racing as the interaction with the scarred-wing avro replayed in my mind. *Why did I do that? Why was I so reckless?*

My nerves twitched in a way that forced my fingers to curl into my palm. The anger inside me was burgeoning by the second. Twenty-nine days ago, those wretched beings had not only killed my parents, but taken Osouf, the only family I had left.

I'll find my brother, and make the monster responsible for his disappearance pay.

That thought sent a wave of heat through my body. Avros were disgusting creatures. The way they used their dark powers to get inside the humans' minds was awful. But avros could do more than manipulate human emotions. Humans could become avros when the darkness took over completely. It was like a plague with no cure.

One way or another, this war has to end.

His hands clasped together, Cylus took a deep breath. "Lorraine, I am *this* close to kicking you out of the pack." His fingers created a tiny space between them, giving me a visual.

"Cylus," Alden interrupted. The old man gently patted him on the back. Alden's expression was full of love and concern at the same time. "It's not your pack that you can make such hasty decisions."

Alden was right. Osouf was our leader, and all of us, including Cylus, clung to hope that he was still alive.

"We're a family," Alden continued, "and we have all made our fair share of mistakes." The elder Sairen gave me a stern look. "I do hope you've learned from this incident."

I looked away. Sometimes I wished Alden was in charge, but he refused because of his old age, and because he said it would be good for Cylus to have some experience leading.

My gaze landed on the Healy siblings. Shariee and her brother were pretending to play a game they had invented involving pebbles, while listening to the unfolding drama. I suppressed a smile as Shariee hushed her brother when he asked if they could play a real game.

Cylus paused for a brief moment before continuing his rampage. "I cannot deny that we need you, Lorraine. You are the strongest and fiercest in the pack, but you are completely reckless." Cylus made a clicking sound between his tongue and the side of his cheek, shaking his head disapprovingly. His voice rose. "A bold and rare white Sairen wolf you may be, but you are worthless to us if you make rash decisions that can get us killed."

I couldn't look him in the eyes. I knew all too well that he was right. As a white wolf, I was expected to have great strength and endurance. Not to mention the ability to Spark—a mysterious, powerful magic that resembled electricity. Sairen wolves considered Sparking a gift from Neriah—a name given to the Light. Though, I had never seen it, I was taught to believe in Neriah. The Light was what made us Sairens after all. But I'd never learned how to Spark.

I hadn't meant to run ahead of the pack, to make my own decisions and let a child die. The weight of my failure anchored inside my chest. It was all too much.

I was desperate for answers. Not only so I could find my brother, but so we could end this war on humanity once and for all. Yet, I couldn't deny that revenge sounded very enticing right now. At times it was a fury that ran rampant beneath my skin.

My legs grew stiff as I stood, glaring back up at Cylus. Shariee blew out a breath as the runt began to nervously whistle. Something about the way Cylus looked at me, his eyes squinting, had me lifting the corner of my upper lip and flaring my nostrils. My mood shifted from somber to sour. The uncontrollable fire that raged in my stomach wiggled its way into my chest.

"Do you even understand what I'm going through right now?" I stomped my foot against Alden's wooden floor. "Don't you realize that every day we don't find Osouf means there's a greater chance we'll find him dead? Don't you get it?" My fists clenched. I searched his eyes for a trace of empathy. "They killed my father out of spite, and my mother was murdered right in front of me. All I have left is my brother. You just—"

"Enough!" Cylus shouted. His hand smashed into the plastered wall beside us. He yanked his fist out, breathing heavily. He moved closer to me till I could feel the heat from his body, his big, rounded nose only inches from my face. "You have no idea," he said through a clenched jaw.

"Guys, please. Let's not do this," Shariee begged as she moved away from the dining table, cautiously approaching us.

My mouth fell open, and I was ready to defend my actions once more, but I was interrupted by Alden's loud slurping. His hand was unsteady as he carefully brought his mug to his lips for another drink, his gaze on the hole in the wall. He must have boiled the water while we were arguing.

The room went silent. All of us watched as he leisurely took another sip from his mug. Without a word, Cylus moved to the leather couch, cupping his face with one hand. He appeared deep in thought.

"Let's have a seat, shall we?" Alden waved his hand, inviting all of us, including Luke, to gather together on the sofas. I reluctantly obeyed.

"Oh, boy," Luke grumbled. His long, scrawny arms swayed at his sides as he got up from the table to join us. Surprisingly, the runt chose to sit beside me. He ran his fingers through his tangled blonde curls and blinked uncomfortably with his long lashes.

"Everyone here has lost a loved one," Alden began. "But we must maintain a united front." Alden held out a fist, his entire arm shaking. Before Alden could get another word out, a burst of enthusiasm filled the room from our youngest pack member.

"Yeah!" he shouted. "We'll get 'em, Alden, don't you worry." Luke's scrawny arms waved in the air, mirroring our wise old friend. I glanced at Shariee, whose face was planted in the palm of her hand, her cheeks flushed. She snatched her brother's arm and commanded him to sit down and behave.

"I worry about the way we perceive things," Alden said softly, the wrinkles in his forehead squished together.

"What do you mean?" Shariee questioned, chewing on her nails. It was a bad habit for her, one we'd all tried to help with. Tearing a Sairen's nails too close to the skin caused pain when transforming.

Alden didn't respond. He gulped his remaining tea instead. Cylus stiffened in his seat.

A scent carried into the cabin from outside. An avro. Straightening and sniffing out the creature's whereabouts, I grimaced as the smell became more pungent.

Alarmed, I stood. "Alden."

But I was ignored.

"When the king comes," he began, "things will change."

Glaring, I shifted in Alden's direction. What was he talking about? *The old Sairen wolf prophecy?* As if Cylus understood, he nodded, then turned his gaze on Alden.

"The king?" He made a tsking sound. "I've been hearing about this powerful 'Sairen wolf king' for years," he scoffed. "Generations have been waiting on this prophecy. Not to mention the newer prophecy from thirty years ago about a 'red wolf'."

I was relieved that Cylus and I were on the same page for once. But I couldn't stop thinking about the avro nearby. It would be odd for one to approach a pack of Sairen wolves on its own; maybe that was the reason no one else seemed troubled by it. One avro was no match for the five of us.

Cylus's tongue grew sharp. "If the prophecy is real, where is he? Don't just sit there and mumble nonsense, Alden." He sank deeper into his chair. "After Arah murdered all those born under a blood moon, who is to say he hadn't killed the so-called red wolf?" Something lingered in his eyes, as if he drifted into a haunted past. The entire cabin grew still. I refocused on the subtle sounds outside. The creature was closer now.

"The king is real, and he has finally come. His name is Ezrai, and he'll make himself known in due time." Alden said. The room filled with disbelief.

"I've never even heard of these prophesies." Luke shrugged. All eyes blinked in his direction. Luke poked his sister as if to say,

Why didn't you tell me? Shariee rolled her eyes.

A soft chuckle escaped me as I studied them in the corner of my eye. I couldn't help it. Their brother-sister dynamic yanked the chains around my heart. I forcefully coughed, switching everyone's attention back to more important matters.

All ears perked as the avro finally reached the cabin. Too casually, Alden held up his hand, a gesture for us to stand down. He didn't seem bothered at all. I glowered at him as he got up. The old man opened the door with leisure, as if the monster was any typical guest. The room was filled with blank stares.

The beast was escorted by another Sairen wolf who remained in his human form. *How did I not notice his scent before?*

I readied my arm, tensing my wrist to move at a moment's notice—to allow the magic in my blood to mold me into my warrior wolf form.

"Dasan," Alden greeted the Sairen newcomer. "I assume this is the avro you told me about." The Sairen wolf, in his human form, gave a confirming nod and then glanced over his right shoulder. The man's forehead was wrinkled and he had dark wavy hair that fell just an inch past his narrow jawline. Even from where I stood, I could see one small group of grey hairs in his mustache.

"This is Evan," the older gentleman said, indicating the avro.

I flinched, but not enough to change shape. Sitting back down, I tried to keep myself in check. *These monsters have names?* As Alden opened the door wider and invited them in, Cylus picked up a chair, placed it by my side of the couch, and sat in it. It was unheard of, an avro with a name. A human name. Once a person became one of them, they were no longer themselves. But "Evan" almost seemed...*human.*

Observing him more closely, I not only noticed his dark-brown eyes, but the lighter spots on his skin—as if he weren't entirely transformed.

"Lorraine." In a low, solemn tone, Cylus interrupted my thoughts. He began to chide me, "If you do anything stupid, I will not hesitate to stop you."

Little did he know my curiosity kept me at bay. Of course, my initial reaction was one of disgust, but the more I tried to distinguish Evan's intentions, the more I felt awestruck. Somehow, he'd taken the shape of an avro while having the appearance of still being human.

"You don't find this odd?" I whispered back.

Cylus nodded in agreement, but kept his eyes locked on the two strangers.

Ignoring the mystery at hand, Luke jumped up. "So, who's keeping guard tonight?" He was immediately hushed by his sister as the rest of us listened to the avro speak.

"I–I, uh." Evan ran his hands through his greasy dark hair. His facial features resembled that of a crow, with a large nose that came to a point. "I heard you know, umm, you know…" He shrugged. "King Ezrai." His voice quietened at the "so-called" king's name. Dasan gripped the odd creature by the shoulder, his thoughts veiled. Evan glanced expectantly at Dasan who looked to Alden with a spark in his eyes.

"Evan here has agreed to help me find my daughter, if we can bring him to the king. Problem is, he went off to a Region I'm unfamiliar with. I was hoping you could point me in the right direction."

My pulse quickened. There was no longer any uncertainty about what we were witnessing. This *Evan,* who acted so human, was still our enemy. An enemy that had surely evolved to manipulate us.

Though still processing what Alden proclaimed only minutes ago, I hopped to my feet. "And what business do you have with the king, exactly?" I emphasized the word *king.* Behind me, Cylus released an aggressive sigh.

"It's not like we've ever met him ourselves," Shariee stated.

Our enemy doesn't need to know that, Shariee.

I couldn't help but wonder whether or not King Ezrai was even real. The prophecy had been passed down for generations about a king who would one day be born from the Light itself. One with great strength and ultimate power. It was said he would lead us to victory over the avros. But most assumed it was a legend, nothing more than a fairy tale.

"Ah, well." Luke had lost interest. His earlier enthusiasm was replaced by an overdramatic yawn as he stretched and made unintelligible sounds. "Good night, all," Luke said drowsily. He waved to everyone, including the strangers we had just met. Stuffing his hands in his pockets, he trailed off to his bedroom.

Unphased by his interruption, Shariee leaned back into the sofa. "Actually, yeah." She paused. "It's a little odd to me too. Why would an avro want to speak to their enemy's leader?" Shariee questioned Evan. Her small, round nose crinkled. "That's just suspicious."

I examined Evan as he looked down at his feet. He took a step back, positioning himself behind Dasan. Next to me, Cylus tensed. Though the anxious creature alarmed me too, I had a sudden revelation. This peculiar avro had more faith in Ezrai's existence than I did.

ALL EYES WERE ON EVAN, WHO HID HIMSELF FURTHER BEHIND Dasan's back. The shy creature's large, pointed nose, barely poked out from behind Dasan's shoulder as he spoke.

"I'm hoping your king can help me," Evan said.

No one said anything.

"I daresay, you all are making the young man quite nervous with your intent stares." Dasan rubbed his mustache. "As you can see, Evan here isn't fully avro. He is fighting the monster inside."

Alden hobbled along with his cane, moving closer to Dasan, and leaned in. "Do you really know where the king is?"

Scratching the back of his head, Dasan gave a light chuckle. "Ha. At times," he replied. "Last I'd seen him, he was off to the Eelo Region. I was hoping, if Evan holds up his end of the bargain, of course, that you could tell me precisely how to get there."

Alden shook his head. "That's mighty far. Fortunately for you, I've been there once before. I would imagine though by the time you go looking for him, he may already be on his way to the next Region." Before he could say another word, Cylus turned to Dasan.

"So you met him? Why haven't any of us seen the king?" Cylus cracked his knuckles as he looked up at Dasan from his seat.

"Yes. And maybe you should ask yourself why. Besides, he has an entire world to tend to. You are certainly not the only pack of Sairens in Elohi. Nor, the only Region in danger." Dasan looked to Alden. "My, you all look tired. Perhaps I should come back another time."

Alden nodded, and Dasan and the avro left. As the door shut behind them, Alden appointed Shariee and me to guard duty for the night. Since avros were nocturnal, each night we rotated the responsibility of keeping watch. It was technically Cylus and Luke's turn. I opened my mouth to protest, but Cylus shuffled us out the door before I could get a word out.

I kicked the ground with a grunt. Shariee mumbled inaudible words as we dragged our feet around the perimeter of the village of Hyra.

"Do you think we can trust Evan?" she asked. "He is an avro, after all. But, I don't know, something about him seemed...innocent."

Still walking, I turned to face the seventeen-year-old Sairen, unsure of how to answer. Though there were only two years between us, at times I felt the need to protect her, since I was older. I bit my bottom lip, my nerves twitching when I applied too much pressure.

Multiple explanations ran through my head as to what was really going on with this Evan monster, but a part of me didn't want to entertain such thoughts. Shariee would only worry. Besides, there was a glimmer in those amber eyes of hers, even in the dark of the night. I couldn't rob her of her hopefulness. We needed her untainted and optimistic mind.

She waited a while for my response, then shrugged as she pulled her thick, wavy blonde hair over her ear. The heat of the day had seeped into the night, so we both stayed in our human forms.

The past twenty-four hours had been brutal. From our failure to save the boy, to inadvertently losing our only lead on Osouf, to the tension within the pack that ultimately led to Shariee and me being on guard duty. The quiet of the night allowed my mind to become clouded with thoughts. Cylus's knotted brows and clenched fists flashed in my mind. Shaking my head, I took a deep breath.

"You know what, let's walk over to the cliffs. Clear our heads."

Shariee nodded.

The rippling of the lake faded as we ventured further away from the cabin. The world fell completely silent and a warm breeze hugged my skin. Shariee gathered her golden locks with the hair tie she kept around her wrist. She fastened her ponytail and tossed it over her shoulder. We decided to walk along the cliffside just ahead before taking a seat, our feet dangling over the edge. Shariee ran her fingernail over her teeth as she squinted at the moonlit silhouette of another region a fair distance away. Their population was twice that of Terah's.

"I wonder sometimes," she began, "how difficult it must have been for the humans to adjust." Her heel bounced against the top of the cliff. "Life will never be the same for them now the avros are here."

"Hmm. Yeah, but I suppose there's something about human-ity."

"Huh? I'm not sure I understand." Shariee rested her chin on her knuckles, turning her head sideways as she gawked at me.

"That's because I haven't explained it yet, silly." I nudged her with my elbow as she tossed her head back and laughed softly.

I observed the trees, the sky, and then brought my gaze back to the town across from this cliff, which was not ours to protect—that was Idra Region, guarded by another pack of Sairen wolves. The world was divided up into what the humans called "regions." Many of these areas had a village or town. Our kind had agreed to split up, sending each pack to guard a region, to provide protection for the people of Elohi.

"There's something in all of us," I explained my earlier thought, "humans especially have a desire to just keep going…no matter how bad it gets." Another breath of the wind blew gently against us.

Tilting her head at the dancing flowers, Shariee cupped her hand under one of the daisies surrounding us, looking amused. "I get it." Her eyes locked onto the daisy, twinkling. "Life goes on." She shrugged. "There's always hope."

"True. But I'm not sure anything will change. At least, not any time soon…" My voice trailed off.

"I wouldn't say that," Shariee said. I peeked over at her as she bounced to her feet and stretched. "Something is definitely changing, and I think Evan is proof of that."

"Yeah, right." I snickered. "Avros are monsters, plain and simple."

Shariee smirked a little. She glanced down at her thin arms, her feet quit bouncing. "Oh, come on—"

The scent of an avro nearby interrupted our conversation.

"Lorraine?"

"Yeah, I smell it. Come on, let's go take him down."

Shariee followed my lead, changing into wolf form. Trailing the avro's scent, we stealthily crept closer, hiding behind a tree when the creature paused. Shariee and I were shoulder to shoulder.

Silently, I pointed beyond the avro. "Split," I whispered. It was a common command in our pack, a tactic we'd used in the past.

Shariee nodded, pointing her nose downward, indicating she'd maintain her position while I moved out. I stalked through the trees a short distance and waited for a moment.

"Now," I mouthed to Shariee. Immediately, she moved from tree to tree. She intentionally made just the right amount of noise to keep the avro facing her direction.

I snuck up behind the monster, keeping each step controlled. Just as Shariee made herself known, I leaped at the avro's back. Biting the back of his neck, I held tight until I felt him weaken.

Easy.

The avro fell to the ground beneath me, defeated.

"You know, you're really good at that Split Prey method," Shariee complimented me as we made our way back to the cliffs.

"I did come up with—"

Shariee, in human form again, suddenly froze. Her nose searched the air, then she slammed her palm against her chest, bending forward for air. Her face blurred and a cloud of black surrounded me.

A THICK FOG COVERED THE GROUND. I SPUN TOWARDS THE FOREST
to avoid walking off the cliff we were on. Placing my hands out
in front of me, I stumbled around.

"Shariee?"

"Yeah, I'm here," she responded.

Listening carefully, I transitioned to all fours. I sniffed the air.
We were not alone, and the distance between Shariee and me was
increasing.

A violent cough echoed through the woods. *Where did she
go?* Trying to follow the sound of Shariee's faint steps grazing the
grass beneath her, I closed my eyes. But the smoke infiltrated my
nose, crawling into my airways.

Without warning, cactus-like needles poked my lungs. I fluttered my wings to clear the haze that surrounded me, but it was
pointless. The burning sensation intensified, numbing every
muscle in my body. Tears filled my eyes as I went limp. Low,

muffled voices approached.

Come on, body of mine, get up.

A high-pitched ringing suddenly filled my ears, followed by a volley of vicious barks I couldn't distinguish. I demanded that my legs move. *Nothing.* I could only open and close my eyelids. The barks sounded muffled, like I was under water.

Once more, I shut my eyelids, trying to relax, but then a heavy breath brushed my face. Opening my eyes, I gasped at the wolf-shaped shadow that appeared in front of me. Two glowing orbs of crimson red connected with mine. My head tingled as I was pulled, against my will, back to another time. The scene took shape in front of me, a memory I never wanted to revisit.

An invisible weight pressed against my body. Screaming for dad was pointless. He too was held down by the unseen force from the avro's staff, breathing hard. At the top of the rod was a crooked crescent moon with strands of leather holding the stone in the center. The crimson stone glowed faintly.

My fingers scratched at the dirt beneath me. *If I could just transform, I could…*

My brother leaped in front of us, his wings unfurled as he pushed against the hidden force. He hunkered down, fighting with each step to get closer to the monster. A sharp pain shot through my chest as I heard my father's cry once again.

"Osouf." Dad coughed, extending his hand as he pleaded for his son to stop. "Osouf, please." His voice was weakening. A salty sting drowned my right eye, and then my left. My earlier lunch began creeping up my throat. An uncontrollable tremor took over my body as I was shoved against the ground by the power of the staff.

In the distance, I could hear my mom's desperate prayer to the Light. "Neriah, protect them, please," my mother begged. The ache in my heart grew, for I knew what came next. *No, please…not again.*

The avro snickered as he gripped his staff tighter. Just as before, the tip of the rod rose higher as Osouf was gradually forced backward. My heart pounded.

"Make it stop!" I yelled, still only able to see my worst nightmare.

It was no use; the avro's words continued the same as before. "Which one of you *Sapphires* is the red wolf?" His tone was sharp.

Crickets chirped, and the world grew dark. I could barely breathe. The newest leader of our pack, Osouf, had finally fallen to the ground. His teeth were still bared, but he was a prisoner like us. My heartrate increased; sweat dripped down my back.

Please…make it…stop. It was coming: the kick, the bite, the sound of her swift feet racing to save her family. Mother's paws trampled the grass, a sound I would never forget.

"No!" I shrieked. My voice echoed deep into the forest. As if someone snapped their fingers, my nightmare was gone. The forest was dark and damp, and I was alone.

I sniffed as tears rolled down my cheeks. I struggled to lift my head to search my surroundings. A vague silhouette of a massive Sairen wolf walked away as the fog dissipated. Could it be the moonlight that made their shadow so large? I tilted my head in the wolf's direction, and a warm breeze tickled my skin. I transformed back to human form, feeling a bit woozy.

"Hello?" I said, as if he or she could hear me.

But the wolf was gone.

A warm hand grabbed my shoulder. Though it was a gentle touch, I jolted forward, forcing the hand to let go. My back stiffened. Still tense, I swung around to face the stranger.

Radiant blue eyes stared back, bright in contrast with the black sky. What kind of magic was this? The scent of Sairen wolf blood lingered, but the newcomer stood there in his human form. He had on Terah's black uniform with the Sairen pendant attached—a crescent moon at the center of a triangular knot.

Neither of us said a word for several seconds. Avoiding the magical glint in his gaze, I broke eye contact, noticing the black strands of hair that hung over his brow. A corner of his mouth pulled towards his ear in a half smile and revealed a dimple on his right cheek. My eyes trailed back to his—a hint of solitude flowed from the glow in them. A wave of calm washed over me, making me feel…lighter.

Once the blue glow had faded, emerald-green eyes gleamed at me. "Hey there." He extended his hand.

Ignoring his greeting, I glared at him, waiting for an explanation. "What are you?" I demanded coldly.

His arm gradually fell back to his side. "What do you mean? I'm a Sairen wolf, just like you."

"Oh, come on, don't act like you don't know what I'm talking about." I crossed my arms and scoffed at his acting skills.

He scratched his head for a moment, and then his eyes lit up. "Ah, you mean a Shilo?"

"I'm sorry, a what?" I asked, noticing a subtle shine coming through the trees. Was morning already here?

"A Shilo. How do you think I lifted the poisonous fog from your brain?" He tapped his finger on my forehead. "Shilos are Sairen wolves with the power to heal your mind."

My body tensed and I swatted away his hand. His broad shoulders straightened as he drew himself up. His arms dangled at his side with hands partially curled into fists.

The stranger studied me, tracing his middle finger with his thumb. There was a twinkle in his eyes that made him seem almost…innocent. I couldn't explain it. I felt safe and relaxed, full of a peace I hadn't felt in a while.

But a *Shilo? What sorcery is this?* I shook my head, trying to break the trance. *Don't trust it, don't trust him!*

His head dipped back slightly as he raised a brow. "You okay over there?" he asked, running his hands through his hair.

"I'm fine." Tossing him an assured grin, I recalled my search for Shariee. I frantically stepped past him, but he followed me, snickering through his teeth.

"You know, common courtesy would involve asking me my name."

I turned slightly. "Wipe that grin off your face." His face fell, and I sighed. There was no time to entertain him, I needed to find Shariee. *Where did she go?*

The stranger frowned, and I attempted to explain. "Don't take it personally. I have a strict rule. I trust no one."

"You need allies, not enemies, Snowflake."

"Did you just—"

"Relax, I mean that in a nice way. I was told you have quite the temper. Lorraine, is it?"

I gaped at him. How did he know my name?

"Mind if I call you Rain for short?"

"Yes," I spat out. "I do mind."

My response didn't seem to bother him in the slightest. He gave me a blank stare, pouting.

"Are you going to ask my name or not?" he asked.

Heat rushed to my cheeks. My heart fluttered in my chest. For a moment, I replayed the blue glow that had taken away the pain in my head. That magic…a manipulation tactic, probably.

"I'd rather not know." I made a shooing motion with my hand and sniffed the air for Shariee's scent. "Seriously, where is she?"

He ignored my mumbling. "Kiran. The name's Kiran Andris." He paused, giving me an intent stare. His next words made my pulse accelerate. "Your brother sent me."

WITH AN INTENSE STARE AND FISTS AT MY HIP, A FIERY RAGE pulsed through me. Even so, I was relieved to learn Osouf was still alive. That was, if the stranger was telling the truth.

I put my hand out in front of me; any sudden movements would have me on all fours. Kiran rolled his neck, apparently unaware of the fury that was about to be unleashed.

"Lorraine!" Shariee hollered close by.

My ears perked up, but my eyes never strayed from the "Shilo" in front of me.

Shariee appeared through the trees. "There you are." Resting her arm on my shoulder, she bent over to catch her breath. "Where…have you…been?" She hauled in a breath, then swung herself upright.

"Ohh, who is *that?*" Shariee batted her eyes at Kiran. My own eyes rolled. She nudged me in the ribs with her elbow as he introduced himself.

After the simple exchange of names, Kiran was quick to return to our previous topic. His lips flattened and he exhaled. "We don't have much time, Lorraine." His serious tone captured my attention. "We have to save your brother." He began marching past me, in the direction of the log cabin. "The Shadow Sairens will be back."

"The…what?" I asked.

Kiran stopped dead in his tracks. Shariee's mouth fell open. Her gaze swung between us.

"The shadow dog things that flooded the forest just minutes ago?" The green-eyed stranger gave me a baffled look. It was almost as if I had offended him.

"Wait, wait. Can someone explain to me what on Elohi we're talking about?" Shariee waved her hand in front of my face. "Hello?"

"Shariee, you didn't see them?" I asked her, ignoring the Shilo.

"That would be why I'm asking," she said, her tone full of sarcasm. "All I know is, I saw a fog, then all of a sudden I couldn't see, and then somehow I found myself outside of the woods as I was looking around for you. Although I did feel something…flow through me." She gestured with her hands, indicating her body, and then paused. "Neither of you have answered my question."

"Hm. Interesting. But patience, young one." Kiran turned to face the cabin again. "Right now, we have a quest that needs our attention."

Shariee and I watched him stride in the direction of the log cabin. Shariee gave me a blank stare. Shrugging, I let out an exasperated breath. Without turning back, Kiran motioned for us to follow.

We scurried to catch up with the stranger. *Does he know he is headed towards the cabin? Is he another friend of Alden's?*

Shariee scampered ahead of the stranger and hollered back to me, "I'll give a heads-up to the others."

Kiran stilled at the front door, his hand cupping the knob without turning it. He stared at the sunlight reflecting off the brass knob, lips parted. He turned, squinting into the sun as it peeked over the lake.

Kiran smiled crookedly at the bright sky overhead and whispered, "It's been a while." As if the sun heard him, an orange canopy of rays rose above the waters and warmed our faces.

I observed him for a moment, wondering why he was having some sort of reunion with the morning sky. The muscles in my shoulders loosened. The temperature was already rising as we stood there, allowing the sun to beat down on our backs. It was late summer, and the days were warm.

His chest rose as he finally turned the doorknob. The voices inside hushed when Kiran stepped through the door, me following.

Luke slid across the hardwood floors. He threw out his arms to balance himself as he came to a halt in front of the stranger.

Luke beamed. "Pretty slick, huh?" He sniggered as he nudged Kiran, a guy he had only just met, for approval.

Amusement curled the Shilo's lips, but then vanished as everyone looked at him. Scanning the pack, I realized we were all in our human form, a sign that none of us felt threatened. Yet, there Cylus stood, glaring at our guest.

What is it now? I wondered, though I too was hesitant to trust the man standing next to me.

"We need to sort out the plan." The new Sairen wolf immediately made himself comfortable, walking further into the cabin and finding a seat on the sofa.

A familiar aroma slid into my nostrils. How had I not noticed it before? *That scent…did he fight an avro recently?*

"Kiran, you've made your decision, I see," Alden announced, leaving the rest of us dumbfounded.

He gave a small nod. "Yes, sir."

"Oh, Alden, you know him?" Shariee snatched her brother's wrist and guided him to the chair beside her. Shariee's eyes silently begged Luke to make no more outbursts. Luke grunted and refused to sit, but then Alden lifted his cane and pressed it into the young boy's chest, letting gravity do the rest of the work. One thing the runt would always listen to the first time was that cane.

"Got it," Luke said as he moved his index finger against his lips, silencing himself.

Shariee hissed quietly to Luke, "You do know I'm only two years older than you. Stop acting like a child."

Kiran proceeded with a polite yet urgent tone. "As I've mentioned to Lorraine, I have a simple plan to rescue your missing pack member."

"Simple?" Luke asked.

Cylus pressed his fingers to his lips, signaling the boy to settle down once again. Ignoring the interruption, Kiran added, "There are others there that I'm hoping to free as well."

Blank faces filled the room.

The newcomer hung his head. "My fault. Let me explain."

He opened his mouth once more but nothing came out of it. He worked his jaw, fidgeting with his hands. We all leaned forward in our seats, waiting.

"*Osouf and many others are imprisoned by the avros.*"

"Perhaps that's where she is being kept." Alden thought out loud. He seemed to take a mental note of it and then gestured for Kiran to proceed.

Lord—" The Shilo shook his head. "No, I mean *Arah*, manipulated another powerful avro, Korland, to build a place to hold

prisoners while experimenting with magic. From what I understand, their goal is to find a way to turn Sairen wolves into monsters…you know, since we are immune to their natural powers.
So far, as Lorraine just witnessed, they have conjured up a smoke-
like 'shadow' of us, if you will."

My anxiety mounted at the mention of Arah. The strongest
of them all, king of the avros. I'd never seen him for myself, but
the stories our father had told us would make anyone's skin crawl.
According to Dad, it wasn't the creature's massive size and black
claws that made him terrifying, nor was it his stone-like skin, the
color of charcoal… No, it was his eyes; evil lingered behind them,
making the hair on your arms stand on end.

Dad had said once, "If any of us aren't careful, I would think
the darkness could take over from just one look."

Kiran paused before continuing, "These creatures are called
'Shadow Sairens.' They are capable of messing with your mind,
and yes, they can even cause physical harm with too much expo-
sure." He glanced around the room, leaning his arm over the end
of the sofa. "Really, they're nearly impossible to get rid of, but one
thing at a time." He pressed his palms against his forehead and
then ran them over his face. "First, we have to save our Sairen
brothers and sisters."

The walls were spinning. This new guy knew the whereabouts of my brother, or so he claimed. All that mattered was that,
according to this stranger, Osouf was still alive. I nearly shredded
the fibers of the couch, scratching at a seam with my nails.

My thoughts stilled as Alden rose to his feet. He stared for a
moment into Kiran's eyes. He pointed his cane at each of us. "Dis-
cuss." With eager yet shaky steps, he began to move toward the
kitchen. "This old man needs some fuel."

I snickered to myself, understanding he was overdue for his
morning coffee.

Alden slowly made his way to where he stored fresh, hand-ground beans, and began to boil some water over the fire that flickered below an iron pot.

I focused back on Kiran. "So, what do we need to do?"

"Ah, yes." Kiran searched the room. "Is there paper somewhere? And something to write with?"

Nobody moved. The runt was abnormally quiet, probably due to Shariee crossing her arms and giving him a motherly stare. The corner of Cylus's lip rose in disgust as he looked at Kiran.

I went to the room Shariee and I shared, found paper and an ink pen, and returned to Kiran, hesitantly handing over the items. "Here you go," I said, a little too loudly. *Is he really about to show us where Osouf is? Or is this a trap?*

Kiran drew an "X" on one corner of the paper, drawing a crooked line diagonally across from it. After drawing a check mark on the opposite end of the line and adding a few landmarks, he paused. "I'm not the best at drawing maps."

"No kidding." Although Luke had been quiet for some time, he still couldn't help himself. "I think you might need my help; let me see that." The young boy opened his palms, ready for the materials.

Even though Kiran grinned, he hesitated.

"He might be annoying, but he actually can draw," Shariee stated.

A sharp inhale failed to ease the throbbing in my temples. I attempted to hurry Kiran along. "Just keep going, please. It doesn't need to be perfect."

"Right," Kiran agreed. "I'll make this simple. Here"—he pointed to the X mark—"is where we are, and this check mark over here is where Osouf and the others are being held captive. In a clearing of Hanska Forest, about eight kilometers west from this cabin." Kiran drew a bunch of little trees on the left of the paper which resembled arrows. His line zig zagged through them, stopping at a particular spot.

My eyes glistened as they followed the line on the piece of paper. *That's where he is; that's where Osouf has been for the past month.*

Cylus clapped his hands together in a mocking manner. "Great," he hissed. "So you know where he is and you want to lead us there. Why?"

Cylus had always been hot-tempered, but not without reason. Eyes darted between the two men. Discomfort spread in the pit of my stomach. Like me, Cylus could be skeptical, but there was something else bothering him. Cylus's eyes narrowed at Kiran.

"Is it perhaps a trap?" Cylus asked. The accusation sent a wave of heat through the cabin.

Alden slurped his coffee loudly. All eyes flitted to him, easing the tension that had filled the room at Cylus's question. The elder gazed up at us, giving a youthful grin.

After a long, dramatic pause, Kiran began again. "I get that you don't trust me, but what if I'm telling the truth? Are you really willing to sit idly by while Osouf and so many others are imprisoned? You of all people know the danger in that."

Cylus glared at Kiran in a way that made me shudder, his eyes darkened.

Kiran adjusted himself upright in his seat. "I've spoken to King Ezrai himself," he said confidently. "This time, there is a plan."

Cylus leaned back in his chair. "The king?" he smirked. "Hmpf." Hunching over in his seat, Cylus spoke in a harsh whisper. "All I hear from your mouth are lies."

"It's true," Alden chimed in. "I've met the king. In fact..." Alden clamped his hands together and rested them over his round belly. "Ezrai was the one who saved Lorraine's mother while she was pregnant with her. He was young then. But that was when, those of us who witnessed, learned that he was the king we've been waiting for."

My jaw clenched. My chair slid out from under me, legs screeching against the floor. I had kicked it backwards without even a thought. "Why?" I demanded, my voice cracking. "Where has he been for the past nineteen years? And why did he save her that day, but not a month ago? Explain that to me, Alden!" My nails dug into my palms.

"Watch it," Cylus warned me, though passion burned bright in his eyes as well. The tension in the room mounted. It took Alden's tapping his cane against his mug for us to settle back down.

The old man kept his composure, even as his expression soured. My chest burned as he spoke. "Nineteen years ago, Ezrai was but fourteen. He kept himself hidden for when the time is right, while also attending other business throught Elohi. There is a time and place for everything, Lorraine. And that, my dear friends, goes for all of us."

Alden gave each of us a glare, till his eyes landed on Cylus, who awkwardly met his gaze. In a way, I understood how Cylus felt; it was infuriating at times, the way Alden spoke in riddles. Even more so in situations like this. While tiresome, his words were also comforting.

"So, what is it? What's the plan?" Shariee looked as if she would bolt up from the sofa in her eagerness. She kicked the runt, who was fidgeting with his nails and rattling his leg beside her. All he managed was an overdramatic "Ouch," rubbing the spot his sister had hit.

"It's simple," said Kiran. "The building is guarded by avros and Shadow Sairens. The only way to get rid of them all is by Sparking." The green-eyed stranger met my gaze with that half grin of his.

Everyone in the room knew about Sparking—a special power that flowed like electricity and weakened avros. When released, a wave of electrical bolts unleashed and zapped its prey. It only hurt evil beings. While white Sairen wolves were the only ones capable of Sparking, I could not do so. I had never even shown signs of such abilities. And yet, Kiran spread his lips ear to ear confident in his plan.

My stomach fell. I was the key to saving those Arah had imprisoned…the key to saving my brother.

The cabin walls creaked, but no one said anything. Little did Kiran know that I was probably the only white Sairen wolf on the planet who couldn't Spark. White wolves were rare and the only ones known to have special powers. At least, that was what I'd thought, until Kiran came along, calling himself a Shilo.

Reflecting on my shortcomings became increasingly painful as I realized our plan to saving Osouf was reliant on my ability to Spark.

I waited for someone, anyone in the pack to address the obvious. Desperately, I looked to the runt, waiting for him to blurt it out, but all eyes were on me and all mouths were sealed. Were they ashamed of me? Had I focused hard enough, I'm sure I could see sweat forming on their foreheads. Or perhaps I was the one nervously perspiring.

Alden watched my hand glide over my damp forehead, then broke the silence. "Go ahead," Alden encouraged the Shilo.

"Finish giving us the details of your plan if you don't mind, good sir." He raised his coffee mug like he had made a toast and took another sip.

Not missing a beat, Kiran went on. "I understand that the white wolf breed is rare, and as far as I know, Lorraine is the only one for miles. Since this is a time sensitive matter, the plan is this, Lorraine will need to keep the Shadow Sairens at bay, while the rest of us enter the Alcazar through a side panel that is located here." He pointed at one side of the square he'd drawn to represent the prison. "If we go at nine tonight, there will be less guards. In fact, as we enter through the panel, there should be only one avro guard. That'll be easy to take care of." He shrugged.

The nonchalant way he talked about such a horrifying place—a place full of prisoners—gave me goosebumps. I sat on the floor and placed my hands under my legs.

"What's the Alcazar?" Shariee asked.

"The avro fortress?" Kiran noticed blank stares all around the room. "Surely you all knew one was so close, right?"

No one said a word. Osouf was only eight kilometers away? *How?*

"Ah. Well, I suppose it does make it difficult when it's protected by Arah's magic. There are many Alcazars established throughout Elohi. It's a place where the avros reside. The one closest to here, just so happens to be a prison where they are using Sairens and humans to experiment in creating new weapons, new...creatures." Kiran's eyes returned to his sloppy map. "Wait a moment." His fingers traced his jawline. "That's right, I'll need at least one of you on the other side of the building." Kiran picked up the paper, turning it. "If we all gather to the right side and then send one Sairen to walk around the stone wall to the left side, whoever that may be will need to kill the avro guard. I believe we could wait, mmm, about forty seconds before flying up to the roof, that's where the access panel is."

Satisfaction tweaked his lips. "Yes, that's perfect. They really don't expect us to even be able to find the Alcazar, but I know how to break past Arah's protective barrier." Kiran leaned forward. "The avros have to be able to get in and out, so they have a secret word…"

"And what's that?" I asked.

"Est therin." He said.

"Est therin." Alden repeated, his eyes glistened. "It's been such a long time since I've heard that language spoken. How nice to hear it again."

My brow furrowed as I glared at both Kiran and Alden. "What language?"

"And what does that mean?" Shariee chimed in.

"Simple translation would be open gate, but from what I was taught, those words are a more powerful, common command from the world we came from."

Alden tapped the floor with his cane. "Yara. Though our ancient home has many names."

Shariee opened her mouth to speak, but her words were drowned out by clapping. A sarcastic standing ovation from Cylus caused our guest to shift in his seat. Cylus was only focused on Kiran, ignoring the history we never learned.

"A brilliant plan, Kiran. Except for one minor problem." His condescending grin flashed across the room.

"Cylus," Alden chided.

"You're right, where are my manners?" Cylus extended his hand to me, as if to give me the floor. I could feel tiny needles in my hands from sitting on them too long. Freeing my fingers, I pushed my sleeves above my elbows and stood, all the while staring at the floor.

"Is there something I need to know, Snow?"

Fists formed at my sides, but the twitch in my arm subsided when I met Kiran's gaze. It was a good thing too, because I would have punched him right in the gut.

"Call me that one more time, I dare you," I threatened him.

Luke, who had been quiet for some time now, seemed to snap back to reality. "Did he just call her Snow?" He dissolved into cackles, nearly falling to the floor. Cylus grinned smugly.

Ludicrous, the both of them.

"My apologies." Kiran lifted his hand in a gesture of surrender. "I know it seems like an odd question, Lorraine, but I have good reason for asking." He scratched the back of his neck, frowning.

"There you go, the name is Lorraine. Not Snowflake or Snow." The memory of our first meeting flashed in my mind. "Not even Rain, got it?"

I heard a giggle behind me: Shariee. My muscles relaxed as I observed the Shilo, who seemed to grow more uncomfortable by the minute. He dipped his head, an invisible gloom hovering over him.

I shifted the focus back to the issue at hand. "Look, what Cylus is oh so rudely trying to say is…" I swallowed, anticipating Kiran's disappointment. "I can't Spark."

Not visibly reacting, Kiran murmured, "Well, that's unique." In a louder voice, he added, "I've never heard of a white Sairen wolf unable to Spark."

"You're looking at her," Shariee stated.

"Surely you can be trained," Kiran said to me. He nodded and then his eyes flickered with excitement. "I know who can help."

In unison, we all leaned forward.

"Dasan. Yeah, I think he can train you. He's trained in the art of Sparking before. Though not a white wolf himself, I've heard he successfully trained another Sairen some years ago."

"Dasan," I repeated, remembering our guest from the night before. "Alden—"

"Yes, Lorraine, the same man you saw last night." Alden's

trembling fingers wrapped around his cane. "Young man," he addressed Kiran. "Dasan has another matter that requires his urgent attention—the retrieval of his missing daughter. How can we dare ask for his help at a time like this?"

"I have an incentive," Kiran said. "I know how we can find Ella."

Alden's expression was sincere. "Yes, the prison, or the Alcazar as you called it. Evan mentioned it to me last night. Of course, when he shared this information..." He glanced over at me, as if in assurance that he had meant to share this update with me at some point. "I thought it possible Osouf may be there as well—"

"Osouf may be, but Ella is not," Kiran interrupted him. "I met Dasan shortly after his daughter was taken. I've done everything I can to help him. If we can free Osouf, we can free the others, and there is one who can help. She's the daughter of two Sairens that are part of their experiments. She was a friend of Ella's."

"We've already sent Evan as a spy to find out about her." Alden said.

Kiran went silent for a moment, appearing deep in thought. "He might be able to find out something, but the one I'm speaking of is one of very few who knows where Arah keeps his personal prisoners."

"Hold on, just wait a minute." Luke leaned back, massaging his neck. "First you know where Osouf is, and now how to find someone else? How do you know all these secrets?"

Kiran spoke calmly. "I get that you're suspicious, but do you really doubt a fellow Sairen wolf?"

"Yes," I growled. "I do."

He looked away, seeming dazed. "We are running a race against our enemy, trying to defeat him and his growing army before things get out of hand. Telling you who I am or where I came from will only delay us. Because who I am will only make you doubt me. Sometimes standing too close can make things blurry." His gaze flashed at me and then back to the runt. "By rescuing Osouf, I'll prove myself to you."

"Just trust you then, huh? Hmph." A maddening laugh built behind Cylus's pearly-white teeth.

Pain flashed across Kiran's face, but he swallowed, straightened, and made his way to the door. "I will have Dasan here tomorrow night. In the meantime, I'm afraid I must depart for a bit."

"Wait just a minute," I said. "You show up out of nowhere with all this information and won't even tell us about your past? And I barely know Dasan either. How can I trust him enough for him to train me?" Heat radiated from my neck and quickly spread. If this was all a ruse, it would be a cruel joke. I began to march right up to Kiran with clenched fists, but Alden stopped me.

"Now, Lorraine, be still. I understand your concern, but I know Dasan and he is nothing to worry about. As for Kiran, he has his reasons—reasons he will share with us in time. We finally know where to find your brother, so focus on that for now. Let's not lose another lead to rescuing Osouf, hmm?"

I let out an exasperated sigh. "Fine."

As Kiran left, Shariee came over to me and whispered in my ear. "Where do you think he's going?"

"No clue," I muttered.

"Can we trust him?" Her breath tickled my ear. The recent memory of his Shilo powers surging through me flashed in my mind.

"I'm not sure." I noted Cylus's tense expression. "Although, it's never a bad idea to be on our guard."

7

SWEAT ROLLED DOWN MY BACK FROM THE HOT SUN AS I STROLLED through the town of Hyra, locating the market for Alden's coffee beans and other supplies. The town square was almost empty, except for the vendors—the older, fair-skinned gentleman who sold roasted beans and tea; a middle-aged woman running a stall of various goods; and a few others I couldn't make out.

I watched as a particular young lady with her back to me observed the fresh produce. She moved from one stall to the next, not paying attention to her surroundings.

I shuffled my feet, kicking the dirt beneath my boots. I glanced down at the piece of paper Cylus had handed me. The exchange was simple. We protected the people of Hyra and all of the Terah Region. Sairens had been here for one hundred years. Most people of Elohi were happy to give us the funds we needed in exchange for keeping them safe from avros.

Most.

A glass jar containing herbs thudded against the wooden counter. I whirled around at the sound and curiously watched the young woman from earlier. Not once did she glance over her shoulder. Most humans watched their backs constantly. This one didn't seem alarmed in the slightest.

"Keep the change, Charles." The girl rattled coins in her hand before she slid them onto the palm of the older gentleman. A sweet and gentle smile filled his face as he wished her well. Instead of leaving, she twisted the lid of the jar, popped it open, and wafted the scent to her nose with a wave of her hand.

She glanced over her shoulder, and a familiar aroma burned my nostrils. An avro was here. I rotated my right wrist, ready for transformation at any movement. Lowering the jar, the woman dipped her head back slightly, giving me a sideways glance, and said, "Relax, wolf, it's only Evan. Completely harmless." The black waves of hair that fell over her shoulder complemented her dark brown skin.

"How did—"

"Your wardrobe, darling." The woman came closer to tap on my black tunic. "All of you Sairen wolves wear them. Special uniform, is it?" She leaned forward, her expression taunting. "Make no mistake, wolf, Terah's council gave you this special *Sairen wolf* clothing to tell you apart from the rest of us. To humans, you're just as much a threat as the avros." She waved her hand to indicate the rows of homes behind the square.

"Robin." Charles's shoulders bounced, his expression amused. "Let 'er shop, will ya? We both know she can't handle your sass."

Robin stepped away, keeping me in her sights. Her fierce stare followed me as I marched up to Evan.

"Please." The avro appeared to be alarmed by my presence. "I-I…" His body trembled, his voice uneven. "I really just wanted…" The creature swallowed loudly.

I paused to look him over and felt a tug in my heart. He was an avro, a danger to both Charles and Robin, or any human he might come into contact with. The thought caused the hair on my human arms to stand on end. A typical wolf-in-danger response. The avro's pupils dilated as I strode closer.

"Lorraine, please don't hurt me." Evan begged.

All I could see were the shadows that clouded his eyes. The moment I drew my arm in closer to my side, Robin's leather boots skidded across the ground. She grabbed my wrist, flipping my arm behind my back.

I exhaled as I flicked my free limb. Nothing. *Nothing?* Well, I had never really tried transforming with my left hand.

"Maybe I'll come back later." Evan voiced his suggestion to the merchant, but Charles brushed it off.

"Nonsense, Robin can hold her own."

I grunted at the thought. Her grip was beginning to make my arm go numb. *Why in Elohi is our Sairen wolf strength not transferable to our human form?*

"Okay, wolf, er, Lorraine…I'll let you go, but you gotta promise you won't hurt him."

"It's not that simple." I groaned, feeling a tingling sensation in my arm.

"Hmph," she scoffed, tightening her grip. With scrawny arms like hers, how could she be stronger than me? Yet here we were, my arm barely able to budge in her grasp.

Once again, I tried to transform with my other arm, yet nothing came of it. The young woman loosened her grip just enough for the pain to fade. In a soft yet firm whisper, she said, "You don't even know how your magic works, do you?"

Her condescending voice filled me with heat, heat that trickled down my neck and into my chest like an uncontrollable flame. Noticing her grip had slackened, I slid my arm free and whipped around to face her. Not an ounce of alarm showed on her features; instead, she pressed her elbow against the counter of

Charles's stall, looking completely relaxed.

Evan remained at a distance, as if wary to come near me. Robin smiled, a small laugh rippled behind her tongue.

I glared at her. "What do you know about Sairen wolf magic?"

Her brow raised. "Here's a better question…" she began, dipping her head forward. "Why don't *you* know about it?"

My gaze drifted downward, examining my right arm. I rotated my wrist, careful to avoid transformation. A faint glow shone under my skin. I had never seen it before. That glow was never there before. *Why is it there now?*

"What…is that?" My body stiffened. Perhaps, it was the Light magic that flowed through our veins. A piece of Neriah lived in us. *Maybe that's what it is.*

"Change, Charles, take it." Evan interrupted my thoughts. The vendor's eyes were glued on me. The avro slammed his coins down and scurried away, mumbling an apology over his shoulder as he fled.

A weighty voice hummed in my ear. "Lorraine."

Goosebumps rippled atop my skin. *Who—*

"I gotta run. Catch ya later." Robin's soft, dark waves brushed her shoulders as she strutted past me. I let out a huff of air, annoyed. *What an arrogant human.* Still, there was something about her. What else did she know about Sairens that I didn't?

I shook myself and then gathered everything from the list while making small talk with Charles. The thought of encountering Robin again brought a flash of irritation. I rolled my eyes.

Charles glanced up. "You know," he began, "she means well." He shrugged and gave me a friendly grin. "I remember when your kind showed up." He grunted. "I didn't mind it as much. If evil had come, something else had to come and stop it."

"So, you're okay with us Sairens being here? Robin seems to hold resentment towards *our kind.*"

"Nah. I wouldn't say 'resentment,' she's just the type to want to understand. If she can't understand it, she'll get frustrated. Takes it out on the thing she doesn't get, I reckon," Charles concluded.

A robust scent filled my nostrils. While I searched for particular beans, Charles disappeared behind his stall. All that was visible was his cotton-white hair.

I located the coffee beans and stood there a moment, patiently waiting. Once Charles found another jar of herbs to replace the tea Robin had bought for his display, he glanced back up at me.

"Oh, sorry about that," he said. Charles held the change over my hand without letting go as he examined me. Wide-eyed, he gasped. "Wait a minute. You must be Orlin's daughter."

"You knew my dad?"

"Are you kidding?" He finally let go of the change. "He saved me from a ravaging avro."

I leaned over the counter and listened intently to the story.

"Yeah, I was holding my grandbaby for the first time," he said. "Was pretty terrifying to hold something so fragile knowing you got to haul yourself on outta there." He grunted again. "But I didn't have time to run, nope." Charles shook his head. "Your dad came in like a rush of wind in a hurricane, grabbed hold of that avro, and dragged the monster away from us."

The way the older gentlemen reminisced—it was almost as if Dad were here.

The familiar ache in my heart flared again. I'd always known Dad was a well-respected Sairen wolf, but hearing the story from a civilian gave me new admiration for him. I had taken my father for granted when he was alive. My chest filled with joy, but it vanished quickly, replaced by a pricking of tears in my eyes.

Sniffling, I glanced back up at the vendor. "There's no easy way to say this, but he passed."

Charles blinked in disbelief. "You can't tell me he's not still alive." Taking a step back, he plopped himself on a stool behind him, folding his arms. "He seemed more capable than any other Sairen wolf I've ever seen. If he's gone, what hope is there for the rest of us?"

His tone was edged with despair. "I'm not gonna lie, your dad gave me hope. Never seen a Sairen wolf take out an avro so easily. He had me believing he could wipe them all out, and eventually we'd be able to return to normal." Charles rested his chin in his hand. "I guess I've never seen many Sairen wolves in action, though." He met my gaze, coming back to himself. "Surely, you're all capable, right?"

"We're certainly qualified." I nodded, grinning.

"Would you mind telling me what happened?"

I froze. My lips parted. *I walked right into that one.* I mulled over my words carefully. It wouldn't be in this innocent man's best interest for me to share the details of higher-powered avros and magical staffs.

I tapped the counter in a repetitive pattern to soothe my nerves. Taking in a deeper breath, I managed to speak. "I'm not sure I fully understand what happened." I stopped tapping and gripped my wrist instead. "He was in a vulnerable state, I suppose. His family was trapped, and my mom, well…" I trailed off, unable to finish the sentence.

"Is…she gone too?" he hesitated to ask.

I bowed my head. "Yeah, she's gone. I think anger clouded my dad's judgment in that moment, and I guess that's what…uh, you know."

I couldn't do it. Saliva trickled down the wrong pipe, causing me to choke. In between coughs, I gathered the bags in front of me and breathed deep. "Excuse me, but I must run."

With Alden's coffee and the other supplies in hand, I rushed back to the cabin, forcing the remaining liquid from my lungs with each cough. The image of that midsummer afternoon kept flashing through my mind. Mother lying limp and lifeless in front of us, Osouf claiming to be the red wolf so they'd leave our family alone, and then Dad…

What came next pierced my heart; the more I replayed the memories, the more they stung. I could still hear the screeching force of the staff crushing Dad's body until Osouf claimed to be the red wolf, causing the avro to take him instead.

I halted as the memory became a little clearer. "That's right," I whispered out loud as the realization hit me. Though weak from fighting against the avro's staff, Dad had stumbled after Osouf and the avros in the forest.

I gripped the bags tight, holding one of them close to my chest and getting it wet with my tears. I straightened my back and swallowed. I had to focus on the now, to rescue Osouf and get rid of these monsters once and for all.

But it was no use. The memory haunted me. I took a step forward and tripped on the uneven ground. I fell shoulder first and face-planted into the ground. A sturdy stick grazed my cheek. The bags spilled over, with one of them tearing completely, but I didn't care. I just lay there, staring at them. A trickle of blood slid down the side of my face, tracing my chin. I didn't move.

"Lorraine?"

That voice.

"Kiran?" His hands appeared in my peripheral vision, collecting all the items that had scattered around me and neatly placing them into the one good bag. He didn't reply; instead, he stretched out his free hand, waiting for me to take it.

I glanced up at him. No smirk, no puzzled expression, not even an ounce of concern showed on his face. Kiran just stood there with his arm out in front of him, waiting.

"You could at least blink; you're freaking me out," I teased as my hand finally slid into his. I pulled myself up while he kept his arm steady for me. The momentum of standing almost pushed me into him, but he righted me.

He blinked. "Better?"

I let out a deep breath, unsure how to answer.

"Why don't we put these away and then go for a walk? I have something I want to show you."

I hesitated at the suggestion. What could he possibly want to show me? "I thought I was going to meet with Dasan soon," I protested.

"You will. Don't worry, he agreed to this." Kiran gestured for me to hurry along.

"One moment. I need a drink of water," I lied, rushing inside the cabin.

Where was he taking me? To my death? I played out the scenarios in my mind, imagining how he might choose to reveal his true purpose. A Sairen wolf working with the avros was something most would not expect. Sairen culture trained us to trust our fellow Sairens—after all, our purpose was to fight evil.

But Kiran betraying us felt almost possible. He had somehow escaped or had been released from the Alcazar prison and knew precisely how we could sneak in and rescue Osouf.

His secrets made him dangerous.

KIRAN LED THE WAY IN SILENCE, HANDS IN HIS POCKETS. THE HEAT made me long to be in wolf form, where sweat wouldn't be an issue, and my eyes wouldn't be as heavy with exhaustion. But Kiran insisted we walk on two legs.

I glanced down at my wrist, but there was nothing. The soft glow was gone.

As the wind hummed, leaves rustled nearby. I cringed at the soft footsteps that followed the sound. They were quiet enough to belong to a small rodent, though none made themselves known. The sun shone too brightly; any human or creature would be wise to stay in the shade or nestled in their homes.

The snapping of a stick brought Kiran to a reluctant halt. His nose sniffed the air around us.

I bit my bottom lip. *Great, he knows we're being followed.*

"Let me guess, Shariee?" Enthusiasm filled his tone, as if we were playing some sort of game.

I rolled my eyes and swallowed.

"Oh, wait…" Kiran raised a brow as he turned to face me. "You asked her to follow us?" Disappointment tinged his tone as he put the pieces together. "She can come too." He motioned for her to join us. The young Sairen wolf emerged from the bushes and glanced at me.

"Sorry, Lorraine, he walks so fast." Her golden ponytail fell over her prominent collarbone as she approached us. "So, you want me to tag along or what?"

I studied her for a moment. Her little button nose and high cheekbones with tiny freckles made her appear delicate. Though, what she lacked in muscle, she made up for by being clever and resilient. Should something go wrong with this vague quest of Kiran's, Shariee could be of use to us.

"We're actually almost there," Kiran said. "Just a little left up there." He pointed in the direction we were headed, to which Shariee's eyes brightened.

"Oh, I think I know what's there, but why…" Shariee glanced over at me. "Well, what would you like for me to do?"

"How about you stay behind, and if we, or I, don't come back within an hour, you know what to do."

"You really don't trust me, do you?" Kiran questioned me.

"You do realize we met just yesterday, right?"

He frowned.

But it was the simple truth. He'd appeared in the early morning after the mysterious fog miraculously vanished, and then claimed to know the whereabouts of my brother. It was a peculiar situation; surely he knew that.

"Umm, I'll just be here then. Later, you two." Shariee nudged me, and then leaned in to whisper. "I think you'll be fine. I got your back."

Kiran scratched the back of his neck. "Well, what do you say? Shall we keep moving forward?"

"Yeah, yeah." I rolled my eyes. "Let's move."

After making a left turn, we traveled beyond the borders of the Terah Region, traveling up and down vibrant green hills that went on for miles. *What exactly is out here?*

Kiran's lips formed a flat line. While his hands remained in his pockets, he kept quiet.

What is he hiding?

A larger mountain rose ahead of us. Once we reached the top, I peered around. Tombstones, lots of them. Gaping, I slowly turned to Kiran. For once, I was anxious to hear him speak; to say something, anything.

I clenched and unclenched my fists in a repetitive motion. It felt like an invisible force kept me from moving forward.

A little dazed, I followed Kiran down the mountain a short distance. He halted, inhaled, and then gazed into my eyes. Why wasn't he saying anything?

I let my eyes wander over the gravestones. Then I saw it, right in front of me…

Amelia Lorraine Sapphire

Spheri feies

There it was, the place of her burial—a place I had intentionally avoided on the day of her funeral. I stuttered over the unfamiliar words "Spheri feies." My vision blurred, and I squinted.

"You do recognize the phrase, don't you?" Kiran's green eyes pierced me.

Why am I supposed to recognize these words? What are they?

Although the sun had begun to set, rays still sparkled through the trees. In an instant, everything around me vanished—my surroundings, the scent of roses nearby, even Kiran. All I could see was her grave. There she was, beneath my feet, my mom. Gone.

This was the very reason I couldn't bear to be here a month ago. Seeing her grave made it all…real.

I reached out to touch the engraved letters on the tombstone: *Amelia Lorraine Sapphire.*

The sting in my eyes only grew worse when I rubbed them. A tear rolled down my cheek and Kiran leaned his shoulder against mine, speaking softly.

"Spheri feies," he said. "Her spirit is free."

Reverence filled his tone, as if the words were dear to him.

"The translation is, *free spirit.* It's a phrase the older generation of Sairen wolves once used as a comfort when facing dangerous situations. An old language that many younger Sairens seem to have lost connection with. The thought is that when we die, we are truly free." Kiran shrugged. "We live on. Our spirit lives on." He nodded, as if in agreement with himself.

I gave him a wobbly grin, then sat down next to my mother's grave, admiring her name once more. As a cloud moved over the sun, the letters seemed to glisten. Rubbing my eyes, I refocused on the colors: pink, blue, purple, even orange, but then the colors faded as the sun reappeared.

"If you think that's cool, you should see the graveyard at night."

Leaping up, I stumbled backwards. My eyes widened. "You mean, I didn't just imagine that? What…what was that?"

"To be quite honest, I'm not sure. The letters, though, they glow at night. Normally you'd expect a dull-grey graveyard, but this place is quite beautiful when the sun goes down."

"We should come back when it gets dark," I suggested. His smile faded and I cringed at myself. A warmth filled my cheeks. "Actually, I can come on my own. No need for you to tag along."

Kiran's eyes steered away from me. "Lorraine, I brought you here to show you something."

Him saying my real name for the first time didn't sit right. I tilted my head like a dog trying to understand a peculiar sound. Clearing my throat, I tucked my hair behind my ear. "My mother's grave, right?" I looked around to be sure I wasn't missing something and then spotted Dad's grave right next to Mom's.

Orlin Sapphire

"I see it, right here. Thank you." Tears once again pricked my eyes. "It's difficult to see, I must admit, but it gives me some closure."

"Well, that's only part of it."

"Okay, so what then?" I asked.

Kiran looked to the sky.

"Um, hello? Are you going to fill me in?"

Shading his eyes from the bright sun, he watched a cloud. "Perhaps nighttime would have been—oh wait, almost there," he said as the large cloud began to cover the sun.

I glared at him and opened my mouth, but before I could get a word out, a shadow fell over us.

"Look," he breathed.

I rolled my eyes. "You know," I began with a hint of agitation, "your cryptic ways aren't charming; really, they're plain annoying."

Kiran smirked. A rogue strand of hair fell over his brow. "And you're just plain mean." His tone hinted at displeasure, but he let out a soft snicker. "Focus, Rain. What do you notice about your father's tombstone?"

Conflicted at his renewed use of nicknames, I studied his posture. His arms dangled at his sides, and a slight frown creased his face. Not the kind that expressed sadness or disapproval, rather a notion of holding in laughter.

I clenched my teeth. "I thought we discussed the name thing."

His expression went from amused to indifferent. "Would you like to know why I call you that?"

For a moment, I debated whether or not his 'why' mattered.

Was there ever a good reason to call someone anything other than their actual name? Sure, maybe in affection, but we didn't know each other that well. In fact, the thought made me shiver.

"Never mind," I said. "You asked me to look over Dad's tombstone?"

Again, I gazed over his grave—there it was, in plain sight. But—

"Wait," My heart thumped against my ribs as I noticed what he meant. "Why…"

I couldn't spit out the words. Instead, my mouth gaped open as Mom's name lit up again, and Dad's didn't. Nothing, not even a flicker of color.

"Dad's grave…what does that mean?" My eyes widened. "Is he…?"

"I'm not saying he is alive, but one thing's for sure, the letters on his stone aren't lighting up. I was always told each name was somehow connected to a Sairen's spirit." He glanced over all the tombstones, lips tightening. "I've never seen this happen before. All the other graves light up."

Unsure of what to do with this new information, I crossed my arms. Cicadas buzzed close by, and frogs croaked. We were losing the daylight. But it didn't matter. Something was bubbling up in my chest.

Hope.

Hope can be a dangerous thing.

"What exactly am I supposed to do with this information?" My inquiry came out more heated than I intended, but I remembered making it to the woods where dad chased after Osouf and finding him lifeless. I threw my hands in the air. "What gives you the right?" Pointing a shaky finger at him, I continued, "What gives you the right to show up unannounced, to claim a month after Osouf's kidnapping that you know where my brother is? Why bring me here and give me some sort of false hope about my father? I saw him on the ground, he wasn't breathing!" I shoved Kiran backwards. "Who are you? Why did you bring me here?"

"Lorraine, what if—"

"Don't," I snapped.

His eyes flickered from green to blue. If I had blinked, I would have missed it.

"Lorraine, be careful," he warned. "The poisonous fog you experienced still remains inside you. It's affecting your thoughts."

Offended, I took a step back, clenching my jaw. "I'm perfectly fine. Some stupid fog won't keep me down."

Where was this intense passion coming from? More words spilled from my mouth.

"Bringing me here was a mistake. In fact, you coming into my life at all is a mistake. Why should we trust you?"

Kiran carefully took a step closer.

"Don't!" I shouted. "I watched them die, Kiran!"

I was weeping now, each word coming between sobs. "I watched them carry his body; there was no life left in him." My chest heaving, I bent over my mom's grave. "Why is his tombstone different?"

The question wasn't for the Sairen wolf standing next to me; it was for my mother.

"Lorraine." Our eyes met for a moment, sending a sharp pain through my chest. Kiran's eyes glistened as they went blue once more, brighter now in contrast to the setting sun.

Flustered, I muttered, "It just can't be."

It was then that I felt it: the poisonous itch that lingered in my lungs and rattled around in my brain. Kiran was right about the fog influencing me. I stood up carefully, more relaxed as I met his gaze once more.

"May I ask you something?" he asked gently and stepped forward.

I gave a curt nod.

"I understand it is painful to revisit such a painful and fresh wound, but the avro that took your brother, do you remember everything he said?"

Again, I nodded confirmation.

"And what was that?" he asked.

His hand hovered over my shoulder, blue glowing from his hand. The mist in my head subsided, allowing me to regain control of my emotions.

Although it was unpleasant, I thought back to that terrible day.

"I'm not sure why, but I remember the avro mentioning our last name and asking which one of us was the *red wolf.*"

Kiran's mind seemed to wander. He was quiet for some time before I snapped my fingers in front of his face.

"Hello?"

"Yeah," he said. "Sorry. Um, right. The avro that attacked your family, is the same avro that's been conjuring up new magical weapons for Arah. I can't explain how or why, but I wonder if your father was part of that avro's experiment. Still, it's not making sense to me."

"And how exactly do you know what that evil monster is up to?" I demanded coldly, crossing my arms.

"I was at the prison with your brother."

I looked him over. If he'd escaped, why hadn't he taken Osouf with him? Why couldn't it have been my brother who escaped? But, if Kiran was telling the truth then it seems Osouf trusted him enough to send him to us.

More importantly, because of my recklessness, I had destroyed our only other lead to finding my brother, so what choice did we have? Kiran was currently our only hope…my only hope.

"Oh, and about the red wolf thing. I'm not sure there's an easy way to say this, Snowflake." Kiran paused, seeming to dwell on whatever thoughts were consuming him.

"First of all, if we're going to be friends, you better stop calling me that."

"Deal." Two shiny emeralds stared back at me as the sky began to darken, lighting up the graveyard. "Lorraine," he started
carefully. Cheeks flushed and sweat rolling down his forehead, he
finally spat it out. "I've traveled around Elohi, and your brother is
the only Sairen wolf currently alive that was born under a blood
moon…he very well could be the red wolf."

9

"WHAT DOES THAT MEAN?" THE URGE TO GRAB HOLD OF KIRAN'S shirt and pull him closer came over me. I didn't act on it—the idea that the mind-controlling fog could once again take over was enough for me to remain still.

"Contrary to what you might believe, I don't have all the answers, but I can tell you this much." Kiran paused to glance over his shoulder, then continued. "The avro king has always feared the coming of the king, but thirty years ago, his new obsession became the 'red wolf.'" His eyes narrowed. "Have you ever heard of Talli?"

"Talli? Is that a place?"

"Talli is a Sairen wolf. He lives with a human tribe outside of Hanska Forest, near the Perri Mountains. I'd say he's in his forties now. A white wolf, like you."

Intriguing, another white wolf like me.

Hanska was a vast forest, and though I'd known of the

mountains on the other side, I had never seen them myself. If this *Talli* didn't live too far west, could we not request his assistance with freeing the prisoners? Before I could ask, Kiran went on.

"When he was in his teens and early twenties, he was known for having visions, dreams."

"You mean like the prophecy about a powerful Sairen wolf king coming and leading us to victory?" I said sarcastically.

"You mock, but the king is truly here now. I couldn't so say so confidently if I hadn't met him myself. You'll know him when you see him...can't miss the red crescents on his forehead."

My heart skipped a beat. "If he's here then where on Elohi is he?"

"Traveling the world. Taking down the Alcazars and other things along the way. Now, may I get back to Talli's vision?"

"Go ahead," I said, tossing my arms in defeat. Exhaustion kept me from questioning it any further.

"Rumor is, he had a vision about a red wolf destroying the avro king."

"So, what does this have to do with me or my family?"

"Well, part of his vision was that the red wolf would be born during a blood moon."

The look he gave me sent a chill down my spine. "Okay, well, my brother was born during a blood m-moon," I stammered.

"Many thought there were no more Sairens born under a blood moon, since Arah ordered for all of them to be killed. But word got out that someone in your family had been born during a red moon. Be thankful by then Arah's plans changed, because otherwise, your brother would be dead."

Trees rustled, and we both looked up. A full moon now glimmered above us. *It was night already?*

"Ah, there you are!" someone shouted, his voice filled with excitement. A deep grin spread across Dasan's face as he approached. "I bet you're ready to learn the ways of Sparking."

The trainer seemed different from the man who had showed up at Alden's door with Evan. He'd been more composed and reserved last night.

His black curls were pulled into a ponytail. Black gloves covered his hands, even though we were in the decline of summer.

Wiping away any moisture left around my eyes, I forced a smile. *I must keep my head up, for Osouf.*

"Certainly, that's why we're hanging out in the cemetery," I teased. "Just ready to shock the dead and bring them back to life."

Kiran's cheeks turned red.

At first, Dasan went blank. Then he gave a quiet chuckle.

"You are quite the charmer, I see." Amused, he put his fist against his chest and bowed. "My name is Dasan, but I don't believe we've officially met."

"Right," I said, mirroring him with the Sairen wolf sign of respect. "Lorraine."

"Alright, Lorraine, do tell me, are you ready to learn to Spark?"

I exchanged a look with Kiran, who seemed to be enjoying my interaction with Dasan. Flaring my nostrils, I glared in his direction. The Shilo pursed his lips and averted his eyes.

I'd lost my temper enough times for the day, so all I could do now was let out an exasperated breath and return my focus to my trainer. But…was I ready?

The poison.

"Kiran," I started. "The fog—"

He must have heard the concern in my tone because he gently pulled my arm closer to him, his powers glowing faintly.

"Just one moment, Dasan," Kiran mumbled in an apologetic tone.

We were awfully close, which only heightened my discomfort. I tensed as Kiran passed his hand over my head. An impulse to shove him away niggled at me, but he'd only accuse me of being sick from the fog.

"Does this thing ever wear off?" I questioned him.

"It normally does by now," he replied.

My brow raised. "Can you use your blue glowy thing and get rid of it?"

Lines formed along his forehead. "Sn—uh, I mean, Lorraine...I can sense a small amount, but I warn you. Once it surfaces, you can get trapped in your own emotions. That poisonous fog, that sort of power...it only brings to light the things that are already there. It grabs hold of those things and if you let it control you, it'll only grow."

"What happens if it grows?" I asked.

"I honestly don't know. It's a new weapon used by the avros. Before the Shadow Sairens, I'd never seen a Sairen wolf turn. I'd imagine the intention is to use the fog to turn us somehow."

"Ahem." Forcing a fake cough, Dasan stepped closer. "Are we moving along, or do the two of you need more time?" The antsy man looked up at the sky.

I searched Kiran's face. *How does he know so much about this new weapon?*

Knots formed in my stomach. He had spaced out again, as if his mind had paralyzed his body. Even if he had a gift to combat poison that seeped into one's mind, could the fog hurt him too? Or was he hiding something?

Pulling away, Kiran murmured, "It's okay to be angry, Lorraine; it's what you do with your anger that's important." His voice trailed off and I faced Dasan, giving a confirming nod that I was ready to go.

While Kiran presumably stayed put at the graveyard or wandered back to the cabin, I followed my trainer for a few miles, to a place near the grey cliffs I'd visited earlier with Shariee. There was a small clearing near the cliffs with only a few trees. The space felt vulnerable, dangerous.

I breathed in the warm summer air. Despite my grief, something about the night was peaceful—delightful, even. The breeze was a welcome relief from the hot summer sun. We were now just a week away from the start of fall.

After a long pause, Dasan tilted his head and said, "Sit."

An immediate rebellion squeezed its way to my tongue. "Mmm," I hummed, opening my mouth in protest, but my teacher was faster.

"Nuh-uh." His finger waggled side to side. "Sit," he repeated.

What am I, a dog? And yet, I did exactly as I was told. Sitting cross-legged, I waited for my next command. The truth was that I needed this, to learn how to Spark. Although my patience was hanging by a tattered thread, I had no choice but to go along with Dasan's shenanigans.

He lowered himself onto one knee. Then he held his hand flat above the ground. A dark cloud floated over the full moon. Squinting, I could barely make out what he was doing. Other than the clicking and rattling of a few insects nearby, the night was empty. No stench of an avro in the air.

For quite some time, he stayed in the same position. Was he waiting for me to mimic him? I switched positions so that I too was on one knee. Sliding my hand over to my side, I let the pointed ends of the grass brush my hand.

"Now, close your eyes."

UNSURE OF WHAT I WAS SUPPOSED TO BE DOING, I KEPT MY HAND steady and eyes closed as directed. My trainer remained silent.

Of course, I wanted to learn how to Spark and save my brother, no matter how suspicious Kiran seemed. I really had no choice; I needed to believe Osouf was still alive, and that we could return him to the pack.

"Do you hear that?" Dasan finally spoke. "There are many things to listen to, of course, off in the distance. Listen closer."

My left eye peeked open to find the strange man still in the same position, eyes closed, right hand still flat above the ground. This whole thing felt silly to me. Meditating was not a hobby of mine, nor would it ever be. Surely Dasan didn't expect me to learn how to Spark by sitting in the grass, just listening to the world.

Once again, I peeked at him, this time opening both of my eyes and glancing around to see if anyone was witnessing this comedy.

Nope. This can't be it. I let out an exhausted huff and fell onto my back. Rocking backwards, I used my weight to roll upright and stand.

Dasan's eyes opened. Blinking, he frowned as he angled his head to study me. The trainer lifted his hand and returned it to his side. "You lack patience."

"Well, why are we kneeling like fools in the first place?"

The tall man stroked his beard, starting from his mustache and then tracing the edges of his mouth. A light humming sound rumbled in his throat.

"You lack the ability to focus, my friend."

The muscles in my face stiffened as I held my tongue.

A light flashed in his eyes. "Do I have your permission to teach you by any means necessary?"

"Wait, hold on…what do you mean 'by any means necessary'?"

Whose brilliant idea was it to have this crazy man show me the ways of Sparking? Ah, that's right…it was Kiran's.

"Yes is for permission. No is no." The man chuckled at himself, then turned solemn. "In all seriousness, you want to give me an answer or keep piddle-paddling around?"

What a hypocrite. I took a deep breath. Maybe impatience wasn't the most desirable of traits.

Exhaling, I said, "I need more details before I agree."

"The question is, how important is it to you to save your brother?" he asked, tiptoeing around my request.

"I'd say pretty important." I glowered at him, hoping to get my point across without an angry outburst.

Dasan made a sweeping motion with his arms, apparently unphased by my death stare. "Excellent." The trainer pushed himself upward, moving closer to the cliffside behind me. "How quick are you at transformation?"

"Uh." My jaw clenched involuntarily. "Why are you asking me that?"

Dasan looked over the edge of the cliff. "Quick, yes?" He nodded, as if in agreement with himself. Dark-brown eyes scouted the area, as if measuring.

"If you must know, barely a second. The same as any Sairen wolf."

A sly smile grew from ear to ear as he pointed his finger downward. He wouldn't dare, would he? I wanted to object, but I thought back to the reason why I was brought here in the first place. *Osouf...*

Memories of skipping rocks across the lake with my brother when we were kids flashed in my mind. It had been a simpler time. Neither of us were old enough to join Terah's safety watch, giving mom and dad a break from the ongoing battle of keeping avros at bay. Back then, Sairen wolves had the upper hand, because the avros weren't as numerous. People didn't turn at the rate they did now. Several humans had even attained a measure of peace with the avros who'd invaded their world.

But now Arah and his second-in-command Korland were brewing a storm—refining the avros' craft of corrupting the human mind and creating new magical weapons. And since we Sairens were outnumbered, the struggle to rid Elohi of these vile creatures had become an arduous task.

Reminding myself of not only personal reasons to learn sparking, but for advantage Sparking would give us in the war, I brought myself back to the present training session. *Whatever it takes.*

I glided over to Dasan. Hesitant, I planted myself next to him, looking down the cliffside. Saliva gathered under my tongue. My heart thumped in my ears.

As I pondered the implications of standing so close to the edge. My body stiffened knowing precisely what was about to happen—

Dasan's palm slammed into my back, knocking the air out of my lungs. I was shoved into the abyss below, my shoe striking a large boulder on the way down.

The wind roared and a high-pitched whistling sound filled my ears. I was falling rapidly. Paradoxically, the rush of blood to my brain calmed me. Adrenaline pumped through my veins. A glow from the moon reflected off the water below.

Now!

Just as predicted, my transformation took only one second. My hands and feet morphed into paws, my attire magically altered into fur from head to toe.

Stopping just over the petite river, my wings flapped and splashed water over the grass. I soared back up the escarpment.

As I reached the top, I found my mentor just sitting there, twirling a daisy in his hand. I landed with a gentle thud on the dirt. On all fours, I strode towards Dasan. I was ready to pounce, or better yet, give him a taste of his own medicine. The thought of pushing him off the cliff sent a ripple of electricity through my veins. The adrenaline radiating inside me burned with a scalding heat.

Wait. Something flashed in my peripheral vision. I looked around, but just as abruptly as it came, it vanished. Dasan was still there, focused on the flower he tore apart.

My vision blurred. Bright-red, flame-like shapes crowded my surroundings.

"W-what…is that?" My eyes raced around the area, but the shapes disappeared, and the scenery returned to normal. A bit worn-out from the energy release, I transformed back to my human body and sat down, leaning back on my palms in the grass.

"You almost Sparked!" Dasan shouted. Had he seen the vibrant flames? "Only one minor issue. I had a theory that has proved true: you allow your emotions to rule you, which is why you were able to Spark after I made you angry, and couldn't maintain the power for long."

All I could focus on was how I had been pushed off a cliff. Then it dawned on me: his insane idea had almost worked.

Then again, *almost.*

"Almost is not good enough," I said.

"My, you are antsy." He came closer and crouched in front of me. "I do understand, Lorraine, I do."

My head drooped. I ached with weariness, making it difficult to control the emotions flooding through me. "No. I'm not sure you do. Not sure anyone does. Why? Why am I so incapable?" A growl rumbled in my throat. "It's not just that my brother is stuck in a dark dungeon, but that him being rescued is reliant on something I simply just…" I sniffed. "I can't."

Dasan placed his hand on my shoulder, searching my eyes.

"Don't worry about me," I said, brushing him off. "I will do this. I have to."

"I didn't finish what I was saying before." Dasan's tone turned serious. "Just because you can Spark through intense emotions, doesn't mean you should. Lorraine, you need to find serenity within yourself in order to control your power. Your brother's life is not the only one at stake." His eyes drifted and he took a deep breath. *Right, for him, this is for his daughter.*

He pointed to the ground, repeating the same instruction as before. "Sit."

This time, I didn't protest. My legs bent as I sat up properly. I rested my hands in front of me, picking at the corners of my nails. The trainer bent down on one knee and put out his hand, which hovered over the grass once again.

"Eyes closed, now. Focus," he instructed. "Try to connect with Neriah, the Light within. The Light is all around you."

"Excuse me?"

"Now now Lorraine, keep your eyes closed. Maybe try focusing on someone. Your brother, perhaps." His suggestion echoed in my head. "And then, remember the rush you felt from having to quickly transform right before hitting the ground. But remember, once you begin to Spark, relax."

Think of Osouf. I must do this for him.

My knee jerked as electrical shocks rippled down my forearms. Static hovered over me, causing the hair on my body to stand on end. The energy flowed in my veins; I could feel it. If I touched something, or someone, I knew I could release it. How long could I hold on to this new power? Surely Dasan could feel it, even at a distance.

My chest grew warm, the heat eventually spreading up my neck and arms. It continued to expand, and all I could think about was how much I wanted to hold onto it. I opened my eyes.

"Release it," the teacher requested as he stood, taking a few steps back.

I took my wolf form. Blue-and-white electricity popped around me. My muscles tightened as waves of sparks ran through me. Should I release them?

A tremor started up my legs and crept along my spine. Something was wrong; I was beginning to lose control. Taking a deep breath, I tried to still my rapidly beating heart, but as I exhaled, the magical electricity dissipated. The spasms were gone, and my body was rigid and cold.

The ground spun, and a tingling sensation filled me. A light breeze blew over me as the flames made another appearance. My legs went numb.

"Lorraine." That voice…it didn't belong to Dasan. *Neriah?*

Everything vanished. The trees faded away, splotches of black covered Dasan's face, and only a ringing in my ears remained.

My heart skipped a beat. Invisible needles poked beneath my skin just before the night turned pitch black.

11

I jerked my head from side to side, and my eyes flew open. How long had I been out? Dasan extended his hand, his eyebrows furrowed. I commanded my body to move, but it wouldn't obey. My tongue itched for water and I could barely lift my arms and legs.

When had I taken human form? *Right. Just before passing out.*

"I do believe that was strange, don't you?" Dasan asked.

I tried to read him. Though his tone didn't seem light, he had to be joking. "Thank you, Mr. Obvious. You think?"

Ignoring my sarcastic tone, the instructor examined me. "What happened, exactly?"

How silly it would sound if I talked about seeing phantom flames. I rolled my shoulders as I slowly stretched and stood, feeling a strained tendon in my neck. Taking steps forward proved a difficult task.

"I'm not really sure what happened," I said. "I had it, right at

71

my fingertips, but then it just…vanished."

He gave me a carefree shrug. With my head still throbbing, I decided not to care what he thought. At this point, I was satisfied just taking consecutive steps without losing consciousness.

"Let's get you some rest then, shall we?"

Dasan placed his hands behind his back and turned to the dirt path in the direction of home. Once he made sure I was safely at the cabin, Dasan went back home to the other side of the cliffs.

The cabin was quiet. Shariee reclined on the sofa, braiding her hair. The sound of coffee pouring from the kitchen was, to no surprise, courtesy of Alden. He was enjoying his ritual late-night caffeine. There was no sign of Cylus or Luke.

Neither of them said a word. I poked my head around every doorway of the cabin. If Cylus or Luke were here, things wouldn't be so quiet.

It wasn't until I heard her familiar footsteps that I realized Shariee was right behind me. I spun around to face her. Braid falling behind her back, she turned her head from side to side, acting as if someone else was following us.

"What's going on?" She giggled. "Looking for Cylus and Luke?" We reached the end of the hallway. "They're racing each other along the lake."

"Figures," I said, shaking my head. "What brought that on?"

"Luke has been antsy ever since we formed our plan to rescue your brother and the other prisoners," Shariee replied. "I'm sure there's more to it, but I don't quite understand what's going on in his mind. Anyway, Luke challenged Cylus and Cylus decided to play along. You know, to keep Luke distracted. I think to let him have some fun."

I could see it playing out, the runt throwing his weight

around a bit and Cylus humoring him. Though odd, it was a quality that I respected in Cylus. He had a way of taking care of us. Not many could be so versatile with different personalities. Yet, he was harsher with me more than anyone else, and that infuriated me. *What on earth did I ever do to him?*

Though, I did wonder from time to time about Cylus's past. We had first met him eight years ago and he'd never once mentioned his family.

Shariee appeared dazed.

I glanced over my shoulder to see Alden reading with a brown mug in his hand. Leaning closer to the young Sairen beside me, I whispered, "Are you worried about Luke?"

"Well, yeah." She pulled on a spare hair tie that was wrapped around her wrist. "It just seems to me that fifteen is still too young for all this, I mean, right?"

My lips flattened, and I was unsure how to respond. As Sairen wolves, our purpose for existing lay in saving humanity from evil. It was the sole reason we had come to Elohi. Or at least, that was what I'd been told—our arrival was well before my time. Dad would tell stories of the world we came from and how one day a Sairen wolf king would be born from the Light with unimaginable abilities and would one day come lead us to victory. According to Dad, the Light gave life to us and guided us to drive out the darkness from another world—the very world in which magic had originated. Dad couldn't recall the translated name of that world, but he called it Yara. Grandpa shared these stories with Dad, and then Dad shared them with Osouf and me.

But the stories had always felt like fairy tales to me. A world of beautiful magic and a powerful Sairen king that would one day lead us to victory over the avros. Ezrai had to be just that...a fairy tale. And Grandpa had been known for telling vivid stories. It was a gift of his.

Pulling myself back from my spiraling thoughts, I focused on

Shariee. Those honey-brown eyes stared back at me with a bewildered expression. I hadn't answered her question about Luke being too young for the war.

She has a point; it's unfair.

"I suppose it's a burden we Sairen wolves must carry," was all I could manage to say. Her brother had made his decision to join us, though he was different than most wolves his age—he lacked maturity.

Just like you lack patience, Lorraine.

"I don't know. It's wrong. For some reason, I never personally struggled with what I am and my role in this war, but Luke..." Shariee's voice drifted away.

Reflecting on the runt's personality, I strived for the optimism Shariee seemed hungry for. "He's certainly a free spirit. That boy was eager to join us. Quite frankly, his energy is just what we need."

"I'm not sure he's fit to be one of us, Lorraine," she replied. Tapping her fingernail on her bottom lip, Shariee leaned against the wall behind her. The blue shirt she wore, a break from our Sairen uniform, rolled halfway to her belly button as she slid to the floor. "I just get this feeling."

"Feeling?"

"I'd rather not say," she said.

I sat next to the Sairen, resting one elbow on my knee and my chin in my hand. As the youngest in my family, I'd always had someone looking out for me, but not Shariee. Her parents had died when she and Luke were little. A human they called 'Uncle' had looked after them until about a year ago, when they joined our pack. Still, Shariee, a teenage girl, was left to look after her younger brother. Now, at seventeen, she had to watch him join an ongoing war. Luke was new to the dangers we faced, and not quite mature enough to grasp the severity of our situation at times.

Wrapping my arms around her, I pulled her into a gentle side hug. "If I'm honest, I can't hold my head up the way you do." Those words rang true, more so as I spoke them. "I had my family, my brother, and I must admit…" My eyes stung. "I took them for granted. And now, I look after myself."

"That's not true. You have us." She paused. "And Cylus guides the pack."

"Only because he's older," I scoffed. "If Osouf were here, we wouldn't have to listen to that harsh and severe tone of his."

"Oh, come on. I'd like to think Cylus is angry for a reason—because he cares."

"Tell you what," I said, ignoring her comment. "Should there be an all-out war someday, I'll be sure to stand right beside you and Luke. I won't let anything happen to the two of you."

Shariee perked up, a hint of concern in her eyes, despite her small grin. Changing the subject, she asked, "So, did you learn to Spark today?"

"No."

"Well, I'm sure you'll get it. You're the toughest Sairen wolf I know." Shariee beamed.

"What if I can't?"

"Don't you start, Lorraine. You will. And if on the slightest chance you don't, we'll still rescue Osouf. One way or another."

"Of course," I said as we stood, and I decided it was time for bed.

Dad's unlit tombstone still on my mind, I stared up at the ceiling, fighting to keep my eyelids from drooping. I couldn't really see anything because the room was pitch black. But even in the darkness, my memories of Dad running after Osouf into the woods and the events that followed were painfully vivid.

"No," I whispered to myself to keep from waking Shariee, who shared the double bed. *Cylus did a thorough check, read Dad's pulse—there was none. Cylus is a frustrating individual, but he would never lie about such a thing. Would he?*

I covered my mouth and glanced over at Shariee beside me. If she hadn't radiated warmth, one would think she was dead. She was silent as a mouse and her limbs appeared lifeless as they sprawled out. I envied Cylus at that moment. To have your own room without sharing a bed…without having to push the full weight of a person over to their side…

As much as I tried to fight it, my eyes became heavy. But even as I fell asleep, the nightmare remained foremost in my mind…

12

As the wretched monsters dragged Osouf's limp body into the forest, my father found the strength to get up. Favoring his left leg, he ran towards them.

"Lorraine, get up!" Cylus demanded.

The avro who had held me down with his staff was gone now, allowing me to move freely.

"Where have you been?" I mumbled, frustrated Cylus hadn't come sooner.

"Get up."

There was a purple glow ahead, which quickly faded. With an exasperated breath, I pulled myself up and, in wolf form, followed Cylus around the side of the lake and into Hanska Forest. In an instant, jet-black fur shimmered beside me. Cylus's wolf form was wonderfully terrifying—dark as the night, standing taller than most of our kind, with broad, muscular shoulders. Osouf had similar characteristics, the only difference being the white tip of my brother's tail.

Red eyes surrounded us, but remained at a distance as we caught up to Dad and the avro who stood over him. Osouf and the other avros were gone, including the avro with the staff.

"Orlin?" Cylus coughed, straining to keep poised.

Although still weak, I sprinted in the direction of the avro. The creature twisted around and ran. Sharp pains stabbed my chest. How could I catch him in this condition? I leapt toward him, but the aggressive flap of my wings strained my right shoulder, causing me to tumble onto the avro. My momentum brought us both down to the dirt. We rolled apart.

At a loud shriek, I whirled to see the avro wailing in pain and gripping his wing. Something moved in the trees, distracting me and giving the avro an opportunity to dart for his life, blood dripping down to the claw at the end of his wing. The red eyes disappeared with him.

Gritting my teeth through the pain of the pulled muscle in my shoulder, I stood and transformed to two legs, ready to chase after him.

The tears in Cylus's voice brought me to a halt. "Lorraine."

My legs wobbled. My heart skipping beats, I held my shoulder and turned to face Cylus. He was in his human form, holding Dad and rocking him gently.

Not another word needed to be said. Cylus and I locked eyes for a moment. Reality was slowly sinking in. He pressed two fingers against Dad's throat. Silver eyes stared back at me in sorrow as he shook his head.

A tremor started in my legs and then spread to the rest of my body. Exhaustion, both physical and emotional, took over. With tearstained cheeks, I sank to the ground beside my father.

I inhaled sharply, my lips quivering as I looked over his face. Something was off about him. It didn't seem right that he could be so lifeless. Where there was once passion shining bright in his eyes, two stone-cold circles remained, unrecognizable. Had his soul left him already?

Long, warm fingers curled around my shoulder. In the sincerest tone he'd ever used with me, Cylus offered his condolences. Though, it wasn't for me. Dad had been a mentor to Cylus and his family. A part of me found it difficult to believe Cylus could be capable of love; however, I knew he loved Orlin. Almost as much as he loved his own kin.

A loud pulse invaded my ears; the agony of losing my entire family had taken over. A shrill, high-pitched cry faded into nothingness.

I bolted upright. Sweat trickled down my neck. I grasped the soft sheets underneath me. I was awake. Still, my breathing remained ragged as I acclimated to reality.

I made my way outside, desperate for fresh air. Uncertainty pulsed through me as I broke into a jog. I had no idea where I was going.

Why was I running?

It was morning. Clouds were beginning to gather in the sky, and I could smell the rain. Still, my feet kept going. It wasn't until I glided past Kiran that they slowed.

He called after me. "Lorraine?"

I suddenly realized where I was going. *I must find Osouf. I'll barge in there with this adrenaline and Spark. They won't even see what hit them.*

Kiran ran after me. "Wait a minute, where are you going? You okay?" he hollered. "Slow down!"

My lungs and legs became impossibly heavy, and slowing down was inevitable. By the time Kiran caught me, I felt like I was breathing through a narrow tube. His arms wrapped around me, and I fought him. All my pain, anger, sadness, and confusion burrowed to the surface. A scream burst from my diaphragm.

It felt good to finally let it all out.

Once I relaxed, Kiran loosened his grip and turned me to face him. Glossy, green eyes stared back at me. They weren't blue, yet I felt at ease. Perhaps it was the release of all my pent-up emotions that made me lighter and not Kiran's powers.

"Did something happen?" he asked.

"We must go to Osouf, now," I demanded.

Kiran grabbed my arm while my foot was midair. I stomped the ground and pulled with all my might, forcing him to take a few steps forward.

"Lorraine. Dasan said you weren't ready."

"Whose genius plan was it for a non-white wolf to teach me how to Spark?" I huffed. "Oh right, it was yours."

Letting go of my arm, he patted his forehead. "He may not have the gift of Sparking, but he's a great teacher. As a right-hand man to the king, he understands such powers through keen observation, and has taught many others like yourself in the past." His arms crossed as he smirked. "He knows what he's doing."

"Then new plan. We barge into the prison and take what's ours."

"That's quite the plan you got there." He sniggered. The more I glared at him, the louder his cackling grew. "Don't be hasty. It's imperative to think this through thoroughly; we can't just go barging in there unprepared. Trust me."

"I know it sounds idiotic." Unamused, I waited for him to settle down. "There's strategy and there's timing. I really don't want to keep waiting. Every day, I wonder if he'll still be alive by the time we're ready to strike. Is there no other white wolf we can call on?"

"Unfortunately, there isn't. The only other white wolf I've met is Talli, and I have no idea where he is." He thought for a moment and then lifted his head. "Last I heard, he was living with a tribe of humans, along the Perri Mountains as I mentioned before. It's a long way from here, and those mountains are vast. It would be near impossible to find him." Kiran made a clicking sound with his teeth.

"Is there really no other Sairen wolf that can Spark?"

"You ask as if I know everything."

"Well, you do rather suspiciously know your way around the enemy."

His grin vanished. "Some things are better left unknown. Don't dig in that hole, Lorraine," he warned. "Look, your kind is rare. It's possible there are others closer, but I only know of Talli." Kiran placed his chin in his hand, thinking. "Sure, let me just go locate the king for you." Sarcasm laced his tone.

Scrutinizing him, I crossed my arms. "Do that, then."

"Whatever you say, Rain." He flashed a grin.

"Wipe it," I said, frowning at his mischievous smile. "I thought we had a deal on the names?" Clenching my teeth, I gave in to my curiosity. "You know what? Fine…" Prying open my jaw, I asked, "Why do you keep calling me by these nicknames?"

This time, his smile spread wide. Kiran leaned in and paused, as if for dramatic effect. "Osouf told me to."

"Osouf, what? He—"

"Yes. He wanted me to do it. Said it would get on your nerves." He observed me, turning his head from side to side with delight. His cheeks bulged with restrained amusement.

Tension formed in my temples. Grunting, I scanned around us. "Why, that—" Forgetting which direction I was headed before, I raised my fist threateningly. "Don't call me those again."

Kiran laughed harder. Heat filled my neck and spread to my cheeks. The warmth infiltrating my chest gave me a little relief from the anger. *It was Osouf's idea.* Kiran's mirth was catching, and I started to giggle.

We laughed together for a moment, until Kiran patted his stomach and hunched over to let out a contented sigh. "I'll have to thank your brother later. This banter gave me a good laugh. Something I don't think I've had in quite some time." His eyes landed on mine. "Or maybe I should thank you. It wouldn't have been so fun if you hadn't reacted the way you did." Only one corner of his mouth slid upward in his customary grin.

"He knows exactly how to get under my skin," I said, nodding. "That tyrant. I'm so gonna get him when I see him." I shook my fist.

Kiran pursed his lips, as if trying to suppress a smile.

Narrowing my eyes at him, I shook my head. As his posture slumped, something clicked. "So, I guess it's true. My brother really did send you. So, he's okay? If you've seen him and talked to him, how was he doing when you left? How did you escape and he didn't?"

"He's…alright."

"Just alright?" My mind raced as I comprehended the different possibilities.

"Lorraine," Kiran said softly. "He's in a prison controlled by a powerful avro. Thankfully, not Arah himself, but Korland is still a formidable enemy. What did you expect me to say?"

"If anyone could escape a prison, I'd expect Osouf to do so, not you."

His eyelids drooped as the rest of his body stilled. "Right." He stiffened. Those green eyes pierced me with guilt.

"Look, I'm sorry. Can you blame me? He is my brother, after all."

I searched out his gaze, wanting him to straighten and grin back at me. But Kiran was lost again to his thoughts.

"My point is," I said, "you coming out of nowhere and telling me my brother sent you had me skeptical. You were a stranger to me, and I'm still trying to figure you out."

Kiran turned his head away from me.

"But maybe, just maybe, I was wrong to judge you so quickly…Neriah's power flows through you as a Sairen wolf, after all. But I still want to know how you could escape an avro prison but leave behind Osouf—"

His palm shot up, cutting me off. "You have every right to not trust me," he said. "Look. My past isn't pretty, but if you believe that someone can change, that someone can become…*new*, then do me a favor. Don't look behind me. But as for your question—I wasn't always a Sairen wolf."

If I had blinked, I would have missed his fleeting frown. It sent a shiver down my spine. What was he saying?

He straightened, then forced a smile. "That's right…I was a human who had turned into an avro, and then I met King Ezrai, and he changed me into a Sairen."

"What? How?" I asked. "You were an avro? How… Ezrai can change humans into one of us?"

Kiran nodded curtly, and then turned his back on me. "I'd rather not talk about it. But yes, he can."

I clenched my fists and stomped on the ground with my boot. "If this so called 'king' is real, where in Elohi is he now?"

"We've been through this. Traveling the world, saving humanity, lying low." He shrugged.

Nearby, I could hear the runt blabbering. Luke and Cylus were coming toward us. When they got close enough, I made out the words, "Catch me if you can" and then only one pair of feet was sprinting forward. Kiran walked away before the other Sairens joined us.

Luke almost ran right into me. "Woah, Lorraine, where did you…come from." Luke bent over with his hands on his knees as he caught his breath.

Cylus walked up behind him. "Boy, you are going to get yourself hurt some day. And for no reason," he added seriously.

"Ah, come now. You're no fun," Luke whined, then dropped his head and walked away.

The sun brightened and Cylus's silver eyes gleamed. He folded his arms and cocked his head.

What is he doing? Mocking me?

Worry flitted across his face, then amusement and finally a neutral expression. "So, how goes the training?"

"Fine," I said.

"Let me guess, you're struggling to Spark." He continued, "I don't get it. The strongest in the pack, the fiercest, and yet, the most powerless."

I glared at him, clenching my teeth. My wrist flinched, but I kept the magic from activating.

Cylus indicated my tightened hands. "That there, that's your problem." Unfolding his arms, he placed his hands in his pockets.

I took in a deep breath and exhaled slowly.

"Your emotions get in the way. You get so heated, sometimes I think you could start a fire."

I stiffened. The flames from earlier immediately came to mind. I loosened my stance and straightened. "Don't get too excited. I've learned some new information."

"Enlighten me."

I told him about Kiran, and Ezrai turning avros into Sairens. All the while, Cylus stood there, emotionless. For a moment, we were both silent, until a grin curled his lips.

"You can be useful at times." His amusement faded as his focus shifted. He mumbled to himself, "So he did turn into an avro; I knew it." Cylus shook his head. "He's lucky I never got a hold of him while he was turned—I'd have ripped him to shreds."

I was ready to punch Cylus right in the gut, but I held myself together, biting my tongue, which was the part most difficult to restrain.

He looked up at me. "You may have guessed by now that mine and Kiran's paths crossed previously, when he was human. I don't know much about him, but his ignorance cost the life of someone dear to me." A sadness I had never seen in Cylus before swept over him.

"What happened?" I asked hesitantly.

Eyes narrowed and nostrils flared, Cylus growled. "None of your business." His voice raised. "I don't want to talk about it." Cylus closed his eyes and took a deep breath through his nose before opening them again, this time appearing calmer. "Somehow, he's a Sairen wolf now, one of us, connected to the Light. No heart of darkness can take on our form. So for now, I have to accept what is."

I held my breath briefly before taking a step forward and placing my hand on Cylus's shoulder. I thought he'd shove my hand away, but he seemed to welcome it. A light shone through the silver spheres of his eyes.

"At the end of the day," I said, "we're here to protect people. If Kiran was once human, he was a member of a race we're trying to save, and if this king is real and can turn people into Sairen wolves, he must have seen something good in Kiran. I don't know what happened, but I do understand the weight of a grudge."

"You're smarter than you act," he said, eyes glistening.

"Despite what you might think of me, I'm not looking for praise. Just looking to complete a goal. Right now, that goal is saving my brother, who may very well be the red wolf who will destroy Arah. No matter what."

"Ah, but it is you who has mistaken me. You do not know what I think. You assume, as you do with everything else." He pointed at his chest. "I watch your back. I would give my life for anyone in this pack, including you."

Cylus searched my gaze—for what, I didn't know. Something untwisted deep within me at the sincerity in his eyes. My frustration eased a little and I removed my hand from his shoulder. Without replying, I spun on my heels and faced the sun. Small raindrops were falling from the sky.

Without another word, Cylus headed toward the lake.

I stretched my arms over my head, anticipating today's training session. As I stepped outside the cabin, I saw Charles from the market running towards me. He stopped frequently, catching his breath and limping. He favored his left leg. He finally reached me with one hand on his knee and the other over his ribs. The plump man made a hissing sound. He gripped his ribs tighter, as if that would help hold them in place.

"The…" Another hiss. "They, the m-m-m…" Each word was accompanied by sharp inhales. Charles took a deep breath and then said, "The monsters, they've attacked in broad day-light…lots of them."

A HIGH-PITCHED SCREECH FILLED THE AIR, FOLLOWED BY SEVERAL more. I covered my ears, as I was still in human form. Luke had come across Charles on his way to Cylus, so he joined us in responding to the emergency.

Cylus, Luke, and I charged towards the noise in Hyra. At least twenty avros hurled rubbish and debris at houses, taunting the people inside to come out. Most humans had disappeared, but a handful fought back with their knives and swords. A few were already being turned.

One of the men fighting withdrew his knife from an avro's abdomen when he spotted us. He took a step back, his broad shoulders relaxing. He was a stout man, and could obviously hold his own in a fight with an avro.

"The Sairens are here!" he shouted. "Get inside, everyone." The man motioned for the other humans to follow him into his home. An avro noticed their flight and whipped its head around, making a leap for the man in charge. The monster's claw grazed the man's arm just before a bolt embedded into its chest.

"Think I'll stick around," a familiar voice called. High up in the trees, Robin watched the action from a distance with a crossbow in her hands.

"Robin, let the Sairens handle it," the man demanded. Yet, blood trickled down his arm from an avro's claw—the one Robin had just killed to save his life.

"I got this, Dad, I promise."

They exchanged a quick nod of agreement before Robin's father hurried the rest of the people inside his home.

In a blink, I transformed and sprinted to the scene. By the time Shariee arrived, several more avros had joined in the fight.

Cylus, already on the move, was involved in a brawl with two of the avros that had been banging on doors. Shariee sank her teeth into one of the avros that had crept up on Cylus.

Even after half a dozen creatures fell to the ground, either due to our intervention or the bolts flying from the nearby tree, there were too many avros for us to win the fight.

A painful wailing sounded from behind me—Luke. As I turned around, I saw that an avro had tossed him into the air. The runt tried to flap his wings for a softer landing but crashed into the ground instead. He winced as he tried to stand up. The evil creature's claw had pierced him near his ribs, staining his auburn fur red. The avro moved in his direction.

Darting after the monster, I leaped over the body of another and flew into the air. *What—*

A hand snatched my hind leg and yanked me down. As I slammed into the ground, my right wing bent the wrong way, sending a jolt of pain to my shoulder and down my spine. I forced myself up and bit into the avro who'd prevented me from rushing to Luke's aid.

But, just as I turned, more avros attacked me. I searched for

Shariee, but she was surrounded too. Suddenly, I was reminded of the young boy. *No. I won't let that happen to Luke.*

I froze. My nails dug into the dirt. I watched as Cylus dashed toward the monster headed in Luke's direction. Cylus jumped, barely grabbing the foot of the avro, causing the creature to face plant into the ground. He was about to finish him off when another came from behind him.

A tremble began to take over my nerves. Luke hissed through his teeth in pain. He didn't seem to see the avro get up from his fall and continue after him. I shook myself and took down the avros standing in my way.

I leaped in front of the creature headed for the runt, giving the monster a threatening growl. Down came another crossbow bolt. The avro fumbled around for a moment before falling over.

I glared up at Robin. "I had it handled."

I changed from Sairen to human. Sure, it was a vulnerable thing to do, but it was the only way I could determine how bad the cut was.

Bending down beside the young Sairen wolf, I assessed his wound, which was deep. Breathing alone had the young boy shaking in pain.

"Luke?" Shariee's voice cracked. Although distracted, she had to keep fighting. Too many avros were in the way. At least a dozen of them were sprawled out on the ground, but still the town was flooded with monsters. It was impossible for the five of us to win. More avros seemed to be coming from the west, appearing out of Hanska Forest.

"I'm fine," Luke said to me with a weak cough. "Help my sister." I glanced back over to Shariee to find her still cornered, fighting off avro after avro. So many had flocked to her that I could barely see her.

If I could Spark, would it save them?

Rubbing my hands together, I flicked my wrist, shifting to

Sairen form. *Focus.* The memory of Dasan shoving me off the cliff replayed in my mind—the adrenaline I'd felt, the Spark it had birthed within me. My muscles tightened, but no electricity appeared. My eyes began to water as I stared at the ground. I pushed further within for the power, but it was no use.

Shariee let out a weak cry, and my head snapped around. Luke moaned beside me. Just as I loosened my stance, something tackled me and pushed me into the dirt. I rolled and landed on my back. The avro's wings crowded my vision as one hand choked me, and the other was raised to slash me with her claws. I pressed my front paws against the creature's stone-like skin but it didn't seem to bother her.

One of her wings had let up enough for me to catch a glimpse at the atrocities unfolding. Nearly everyone was held down, gritting their teeth as they pushed back at the mass of monsters.

Still struggling to breathe, I searched the tree Robin had occupied, but she was gone. Surely, she hadn't abandoned us? Her family and friends were in danger.

Desperate for air, I kicked my back legs repeatedly at the creature's stomach. The pressure of her claws relented, but it didn't loosen her grip. She was trying to suffocate me.

Without warning, my muscles gave out, leaving me limp while my head tingled. My eyelids closed involuntarily. Though still aware, there was nothing I could do, until...

A Spark. My eyes shot open as the current flooded my body. *Could this be it?*

The avro on top of me pulled back her hand with a puzzled expression. Electricity built within me. The avro widened her eyes and hissed as she leaped off me.

Pulling myself up, I noticed a shift in my newfound power… it was suddenly fading.

No!

The creature frantically tossed her head in search of the source of my power, but then swung back as I faltered.

I opened my jaw and leaped in the monster's direction. Just before I reached her, Robin cried, "No!" and then a small bolt whistled past my ear and into the monster's leg. I swung back around, glaring at the surrounding trees.

"I had it handled," I snapped, watching the avro stumble and fall to the ground. My ears flinched at the sounds of Robin approaching.

"You don't understand, dog," Robin retorted. As she looked over the fallen avro, her eyes glistened. "That's my cousin."

The young woman bent down, caressing the fallen avro's face. "I'm going to save you," she muttered. There was no response from the creature, only a drowsy eyeroll as she lost consciousness.

Robin scrunched her lips as she straightened and scanned the space around us. I didn't know when it had happened, but another Sairen wolf pack had joined the fight. Even old Alden was getting his teeth bloody. The tables had turned, giving us the upper hand. Yet, the fighting seemed to anger Robin.

Three bolts were attached to her hip with leather, but in a flash, they were gone. *Should I coax her to safety?* Although thin, her arms were defined. Still, I couldn't let her fight without her weapon. Robin wiped her forehead; her deep bronze complexion glistened in the sunlight. Before I had the chance to open my mouth, she spoke.

"Listen up," she insisted. "Those bolts are filled with sleeping medicine. They'll wake up within the next hour. In the meantime, we need to gather the rest of the avros into one place." Robin raised her brow and crossed her arms. "Think you can handle that?"

I scoffed. *She's crazy.* "Why are you so against killing these monsters?"

She glanced down at her cousin, her jaw tightening. "They

were people once. If they can be turned, they can change back."

Kiran. It is possible, but how? We don't know where Ezrai is.

"And what if they can't?" I questioned.

The young woman placed her right hand on her hip, tossed her dark-brown waves over her shoulders, and bent down till we were almost nose to snout.

"They. Will. You understand me?" Grinding her teeth, Robin stared me down.

Admittedly, she wasn't wrong; Kiran was proof of that. But what would she do with all these avros before she figured out how to save them?

She straightened, sighing. "I need your cooperation, if you don't mind."

I spotted more avros headed in our direction. Even with the help of another pack, without any more of Robin's sleeping bolts we would struggle to defeat the horde of avros approaching.

Dozens of avros were sprawled on the ground, either dead or asleep. I spotted Kiran, who was trying his best to keep Alden from taking on too much.

Snorting, I tossed Robin a defeated glare. "Fine. What's your plan?"

"We use you as bait and gather the avros in the barn. Once we have as many as we can get in there, I'll throw my sleeping bomb inside."

My mouth fell open. "Wait a minute. You have a *what*?" I cocked my head. "And what do you mean, use me as bait? Have you lost your mind?" I straightened, then remembered that the avro at my feet was only asleep. "And what are you going to do when they wake up?"

Robin raised a brow, waiting for me to finish my outburst. Her eyes rolled.

"Are you done?" she asked calmly. "Well, first off...we say you're the red wolf, then let them chase you." Robin gave a casual shrug. "We'll guide them to that burgundy colored barn over there." She pointed at the designated trap and then paused as she noticed my baffled expression. "Yes, I hear the rumors. I know about your brother, the whole red wolf prophecy and blah blah blah. But when people are first turned, they tend to lose their ability to think clearly for some time. Judging by the crazed look in all the ones I'm seeing here, most are freshly turned. They'll lose it the minute they think you were also born under a blood moon."

A growl escaped me. How could she talk about such a sensitive subject so carelessly? "What—" I was cut off by her continuing explanation.

"As for when they wake up, well, I'll keep the barn locked." Robin let out a quiet sigh. "Till I figure out how to save them," she muttered.

Realizing there was no other alternative, at least for now, I gave a curt nod. "No time to lose."

"Hey there!" Robin shouted.

Her voice boomed around the clearing, rattling my eardrums and making my back tense. Many of the avros turned their heads.

"Let's do a trade. Leave our town alone and take the red wolf instead," she hollered. Grins filled the avros' faces. "That's right, she's here, born under a blood moon."

Robin pointed in my direction. I assumed a shocked expression with a hand on my chest, releasing a loud gasp for dramatic effect.

I backed up slowly, remaining in my wolf form as I waited for them to charge. Drool dripping from their mouths, they seemed to contemplate for a moment the truth in Robin's words, cocking their heads at me.

In no time, the avros started forward. Kicking the ground beneath me, I sprinted away. Taking a longer route would give Robin time to sneak into position, so I raced around the village.

The avros followed.

Cutting back through the market center, I made my way to the barn just outside of town. As I passed by Cylus, I realized he wasn't fighting. He just stood there, watching me run.

Could every single one of them be on my tail?

I turned my head, slowing myself down in the process. My heart pounded harder as I confirmed all the avros were, in fact, chasing me. Inhaling sharply, I picked up the pace. One of the avros had gotten close enough to reach out and grab my tail.

Robin barely reached the barn as I lured the avros towards it. Once I saw her find a hiding spot behind a pile of wood, I ran faster.

The avro closest to me released a menacing screech as he stretched out his arm. His fingertips grazed my fur. Before he could make another attempt, I leaped forward, diving into the wooden building. I rolled right into a stall door, hitting my head against the wooden rod beside it.

My head began to throb, which turned into dizziness after I made a swift transformation to human form. The avro who was ahead of the rest wrapped his hand around my leg. I glanced up at a tiny, closed window above, wiggling relentlessly towards it, but his pulling on my leg made it difficult to break free.

The rest of the avros crowded in, and soon after, the barn door creaked shut as Robin latched it from the outside. All of them turned their heads at the commotion, including the avro holding onto me.

Taking advantage of the distraction, I lifted my leg and pulled it back. Ignoring the ache pulsating at the back of my skull, I kicked my leg with all my might. The avro shot backwards and fell at the feet of some of his comrades. Every head perked up, looking at me. Using the momentum from rolling myself forward, I pushed the stall door shut and locked it.

They clawed and kicked violently at the obstacle while a few of them began to climb over. As I got to my feet, Robin called from the rooftop.

"Are you done in there?"

The window was open. I stared at it for a brief moment until…something clicked. I lifted my shirt over my nose.

"Done," I replied. Taking in a deep breath, I watched as Robin tossed the sleeping bomb inside. As I rushed to the window, the avro that I had escaped from made it over the gate.

"Where do you think"—his coughs from the fog slowed his speech—"you're going." With his hand out in front of him, he fell to his knees and then face-planted into the ground. I crawled out of the window, jumped to the ground, and then dusted myself off.

Rubbing the back of my head, I carefully looked side to side and then walked around the wooden structure. Robin stood outside the barn doors, taking a few steps back as smoke seeped through the cracks.

Robin pumped her fist. "Got 'em!" she cheered. For the first time, she smiled. The crazy idea that avros could turn back to humans was important to her.

For a moment, I thought of her cousin. My lips pursed. It was silly to hold on to such hope. Yet, her eyes gleamed as she struck a victory stance. I might not have that kind of hope, but I wished I had. At least for now, she still had time to save her cousin. Dusting myself off, I found myself smiling proudly. Robin's wild plan had worked.

We did it.

But what will she do when all those avros wake?

Is she that mad that she'd risk the lives of everyone else around her on a hunch? Kiran claims to have been turned back by 'the king,' but Robin hasn't seen him. I haven't seen him.

I glanced over my shoulder at the barn. Multiple avros were inside, silent—asleep. At least they had nowhere to run.

Robin flinched, reaching for her crossbow as I turned back to face her. It wasn't like any crossbow I'd ever seen. It was smaller and seemed lighter. Designs were carved in the wood—one being a tiny drawing of a bird with a long tail.

Realizing she was out of bolts, Robin grunted while her shoulders drooped. All of her darts were lodged in the sleeping monsters. She sighed. "Right, I almost forgot I have more on the other side of the barn."

At the sound of footsteps, Robin looked up. "Looks like the fun is not over," she said.

I followed her gaze to find more avros headed our way, but something caught my eye—it was *him*. The avro who'd taken Osouf and killed my parents. His fingers wrapped around the charcoal staff, the red stone at the top of it swirling with black.

There he was, the one I'd been looking for, the evil being that took everything from me.

I took a closer look at the staff. As if it were a living thing, the black cloud inside pulsated. Still, I couldn't take my eyes off the shimmering red...it called me.

"Korland," Robin whispered with disgust as she gave him a menacing glare, breaking my trance.

"You know him?"

"No time for chitchat." Without taking her eyes off him, she strode around the barn, and I followed in time to see her grab a brown satchel hanging by a hook. There were at least twenty more darts inside.

"Lorraine." Cylus jogged to the barn. "You must hide." His breath brushed my shoulder as he placed his hand on my back and gave me a push that caused me to stumble.

"Hold on, no need to push me," I hissed.

"I say we trade her for our lives." With a mischievous grin, Robin formed a fist and placed it on her hip. She was lucky I couldn't Spark. Perhaps that's why I couldn't; I wouldn't be able to control it.

Peering back over his shoulder, Cylus clicked his tongue and then stared straight into Robin's eyes.

"Don't be naïve, human," he snarled. "You joke as if that would be a simple solution, but what darkness would befall humanity if the thing they're after is the thing they get?"

Robin chortled, and Cylus and I whipped our heads around. "You mean you actually think *she's* the red wolf?" An involuntary flinch rattled my nerves as she pointed at me mockingly.

"Of course not, but she is Osouf's sister." Cylus eyed Korland's approach once more. "We don't have time for this." He gestured for me to hide behind the barn.

Robin blinked. She rolled her neck and stretched her arms above her head. "Relax. No explanation needed. She's basically a ploy. Got it." She winked.

Cylus ignored her, keeping his gaze on the avros approaching. Reluctantly, I slid around the barn. My fingertips grazed the weathered wood.

I peeked around the corner. The thumping in my chest increased as Korland's features became clear. The past flashed before me, making my blood boil when I looked at his face—those bright eyes in contrast to his black hair and square jaw. I remembered him well. His skin was mostly black, but there were a few lighter spots. The face of Evan came to mind—his human features shone through the ugliness of the monster.

Cylus released a low whistle, gesturing to me. "Whatever you are thinking…no." His tone deepened. "He's coming. Out of sight, you." Cylus shooed me away. Reluctantly, I hunkered down and watched as the rest of the avros gathered close by. The Sairen wolves who had come to our aid went out to meet them.

All eyes turned to Luke, who was limping with his shirt torn and wrapped tightly around his torso. Even through the black of his uniform, the crimson stain was noticeable.

The Sairen wolves whispered among themselves until Luke

was directed to join me.

Great. Hiding with the runt. It was ridiculous. Osouf was the one born on the night of a red moon; Korland had what he wanted. Why would my packmates keep me from facing the atrocious creature that ruined my life? The one who took my brother?

Was Osouf…still alive?

Kiran had finally caught up with the pack, his nose in the air. "I smell them." He paused, turning his head. "The Shadow Sairens."

"The shadow what?" Luke nearly shouted in my ear. The runt sniggered, then winced as he clenched his side. Folding my arms, I leaned in, giving him a stern look.

"You need to be more careful."

Luke's watery eyes drooped. "You're right," he said in a somber tone, his voice hoarse. "Sorry."

I scrunched my lips together, biting the inside of my cheek as the runt sat on the ground. Dropping to my knees beside him, I gently patted his shoulder. "Try to be still, pup."

"I'm no pup," Luke said.

"Right." I looked him over as he tightened his jaw, fighting back tears from the pain. "You're doing great."

My chest began to burn. The urge to jump out and fight was an itch so strong that my legs ached beneath me. Perhaps this was the real reason Cylus wanted me to hide—so I wouldn't do anything impulsive. My teeth ground together as I dug my nails into the muddied grass and yanked out a handful, squeezing the blades in my fist.

"Shadow Sairens, you say?" Cylus answered Kiran. "Does this mean Korland has come to fight?"

"Not exactly," Kiran responded.

Discreetly, I peeked around the barn and observed Korland. He marched forward slowly. Everyone else stood in position, looking uncertain.

Behind Korland and his crew was a dark fog in the shape of wolves. Their piercing red eyes had no pupils.

Kiran turned back to find me glaring at him. He tilted his head with a slight grin and a raised brow. "Are you hiding?"

"It was Cylus's idea," I spat back.

Kiran's eyes bounced from Cylus to the large avro named Korland. The corner of his lip rose as he stared at our enemy. Kiran sighed, dropping his head.

"He's not after you," Kiran said. "He's after me."

15

My ragged pulse pounded in my neck. The palpitations worsened as I watched Korland, the avros, and the Shadow Sairens come closer. Why was he after Kiran?

I stepped out in the open. Korland paused, tapping the ground with his staff, which in turn stilled his posse. Whether he stopped because of Kiran or me was unclear, but we all stood frozen.

"Where is your *king*?" Robin asked Cylus as she tossed her head back, her tone mocking. "Doesn't he have the power to stop all this?" She grabbed a bolt and loaded it. Everyone appeared to be on edge.

"If he does exist, I think he would be here," Shariee chimed in.

Korland raised his hand. Without turning his head, Cylus gave a soft command under his breath. "Lorraine, get Luke to safety." Korland's arm swung down, releasing the Shadow

Sairens. Quickly, I glanced around, looking for a way out.

Wolf-shaped clouds sprinted in our direction. The pack retreated from the poisonous fog. Luke and I were briefly forced apart by the Shadow Sairens, and I once again stood in the open. My eyes locked with Korland's. I clenched my fist against my chest, the edges of a painful memory sending tendrils of pain across my sternum.

Luke's wet cough diverted my attention. With an exasperated breath, I turned away from Korland. Nearby, Kiran stood on two legs with a blank stare.

"Hello?" I called to Kiran as I helped Luke, who must have been knocked down by the Shadows, to stand.

"Sorry," he mouthed, marching towards us and placing his hand over Luke, his eyes glowing blue. A furious expression formed. "Don't worry, I'll take care of this." He looked past me. "I'll heal your friends first." He trudged forward into the fog.

"Kiran, wait—"

But he never turned back. Instead, he put out his hand, gesturing for Korland to stop. Korland watched as Kiran approached, and the avro called off the Shadow Sairens. Many Sairen wolves were already slumped over, coughing to free their lungs from the fog. While making his way to Korland, Kiran made a point to reach out and touch each Sairen wolf affected by the dark fog. A brilliant blue light surged through them.

My feet moved forward in two small steps, but I halted. *What am I doing? Is this really a good idea?*

The urge itched deep within me, but I couldn't just jump out in the open and leave Luke by himself. It was imperative that this time I didn't make any mistakes. *Korland is more than an average avro.*

Luke muttered from his hiding place, breaking my focus. "Hello?"

I shook my head as I turned back to the young Sairen. "I'm

right here," I said. To my surprise, his eyes shone with joy.

"I think I'm going to be okay." He held his side, stifling a cough.

I frowned at him, peering at his wound. "Is it still bleeding?"

"Seems like it stopped." Luke cheered, holding up his thumb.

More noises sounded from around the corner. I focused on fixing Luke's makeshift bandage and placing his arm around my neck for support. Everything in me desired to seek revenge, but I needed to help Luke. *If it weren't for his wound...*

"Let's move."

Every few steps Luke would hiss in pain, clenching my shoulder. But once we moved further away, he quietened. Coming to a stop, I removed his arm from around my neck and noticed the silence.

Following Luke's stare, I watched as Korland and two avros escorted Kiran past the open space outside of Hyra and into Hanska Forest.

"What does he want with Kiran?" I questioned, still glaring at the forest.

"Go ahead," Luke said.

"Excuse me?"

"You want to go after him, don't you?"

"Well, no...I mean yes, but no." I pulled his arm back around my neck, but he carefully removed his arm and lowered himself to the ground.

"I'll be fine right here," he said. "The other Sairens will find me. Now go find Osouf."

"Osouf," I whispered. I bit my bottom lip as the thought sunk in—right now, it was Kiran I wanted to rescue. How did I not think of Osouf? But we had a plan to rescue my brother. Something we'd been meticulously plotting due to the dangers Kiran had warned us about.

Would it be foolish to follow them and attempt to rescue

Kiran? And what about Osouf?

"Uh-oh," Luke whispered. "There's more of them." I whirled to find more of the wolf-shaped Shadows heading towards the rest of the pack.

My eyes darted between the woods and the Shadows. The longer I stood there, the faster my heart raced. A heat spread across my chest and down to my legs. I had to act quickly, and there was no use sticking around. It would only allow the Shadow Sairens to poison my mind once again, and this time, we had no Shilo to free us from their influence.

I'll rescue Kiran, and bring him back to heal the pack.

Without looking back, I entered the forest. Korland, Kiran, and the avros were a good distance ahead. Following their scent was easy enough, but I could also hear the stone clacking against the staff. Why was it loud enough for me to hear?

I crept deeper into the forest after my prey. All the while, they were silent. For the entire eight kilometers, no one said a word.

Finally, they paused at a large clearing. I moved in closer and hid behind a tree.

Korland's voice sounded.

"Est therin!"

The ground vibrated beneath me, accompanied by an abrupt crackling noise. The barrier began to thin out. "Dedrus, go open the latch."

The dull grey of the building in front of them came into view, sending a chill down my back. *Is this where they're keeping my brother?*

Still lurking behind the tree, I took note of the prison before me. The elongated front door was latched shut with black iron. The Alcazar was large, but somehow smaller than I expected. The prison hardly had any character, as it was just a long-drawn-out rectangle with one half of the roof coming to a point and the other, flat. Dark green moss grew between the cracks of the stone.

The grass surrounding the perimeter was unkempt. Some of it was brown, while weeds thrived in patches up to where I was standing.

A musky smell mixed with the stench of avros, making my nose crinkle. I pressed my tongue against the roof of my mouth to keep from sneezing.

Once the door opened, Korland turned to the other avro who remained close to Kiran. "Take him through to the rooftop," he ordered.

The avro did as instructed, pulling Kiran by the arm and forcing him up the outer stoned stairway. Korland briefly glanced behind him. My heart skipped a beat when he looked in my direction. Fortunately, he didn't see me. He and Dedrus went inside, leaving a female avro standing guard. *Where are all the avro guards?*

I picked up a rock and threw it across from me, hiding behind a tree as it landed. I peeked at the female avro to find her turning her head side to side, but still standing in place. Her eyes kept wandering until she finally turned her back on me. There were no other rocks by my feet, so I found a stick instead and threw it with as much strength as I could. The avro's head whipped back. She looked left and then right before she stepped out to investigate.

Once she began to search the woods, I tiptoed out from behind the tree, careful not to make a sound. The female avro had disappeared.

I hoped there were no other avros nearby. After I made it to the prison without getting caught, I pressed myself flat against the wall.

I squinted at the trees. The female avro was visible again, slowly making her way back. I slid against the outer wall and peered around the other side. My breathing wavered when I found another avro standing guard. Fighting was not an option. The commotion would alert others to my presence. There was no way to know how many avros I would have to face, let alone the power of that staff.

I looked back at the avro who had guarded the front door—she was at the edge of the woods now. I swallowed and checked the other side. Of course, another stood watch, but a large wooden crate caught my eye. On my hands and knees, I crawled up to it. As the female avro made it back to her post, she called out to the avro on my side of the prison walls.

"Jace," she hollered. "Someone's nearby. Call the dogs."

"Interesting; thought I heard something too," Jace replied.

Pressing up against the wall behind me and covering my mouth, I watched as the avro closest to me walked past. His arms dangled at his sides. He took leisurely steps, unbothered by the female avro's concern.

"Have them sniff out the woods."

Jace's whistle rattled in my ear, and soon after, the black fog of Shadow Sairens swept past me.

"Search over there," Jace said in an aloof tone, pointing deeper into the woods.

In one swift motion, I leaped onto the crate. Once the guard avros were occupied, I transformed and flew up to the roof. After landing, I laid low, my legs bent as I carefully made my way to the trapdoor. Noticing the rusted hinges, I sighed. I switched back to my human form.

Keeping my hands steady, I slowly pulled the handle. The hatch let out a small protest, and I paused, tensing.

It seemed no one had heard it. I relaxed and spit into the hinges, uncertain if that would help. Taking a deep breath, I pulled the panel open. To my surprise, the door was quiet. Beyond the trapdoor, it was dark, except for a dim light that shone in the center of the room down below. As I slid inside, I closed the access door, hoping nobody had noticed the outdoor light flooding inside. I positioned one foot on the first step of the staircase. Hunkering down, I searched the room below. The dim light was a single lantern, and Kiran sat in a chair with his back facing me. I placed my foot onto the next step and stilled when another voice spoke.

"Is it time?" the voice from below asked.

"No, no. The subject needs more study," a different, stuffy-sounding voice replied.

Gripping the railing, I carefully lowered my head until I could see the two avros. *I could take 'em.*

Don't you dare. A gasp nearly escaped me at the voice in my head, which sounded like Cylus. Biting my tongue, I rolled my eyes and sat, leaning against the rail. A part of me wished he really was here, telling me not to, because the urge to argue burned within me. *I could take them easily!*

My breathing slowed. But then again, Kiran strategically put a plan in place to rescue Osouf from this very prison. A plan that required several of us, and the ability to spark. *But yet, I'm doing it alone, without sparking…*

Why was it so easy?

"So, what're we doing then? Just watching?" the first avro inquired, bringing me back to the situation at hand. I squinted at Kiran, who hardly moved. Was he unconscious? No…he was sitting up straight, his head following the two avros as they moved about.

"Eh, let's go," the second avro said.

After they were gone, I trotted down the steps and tiptoed around Kiran till I could get a good look at his face. He wasn't restrained, but his eyes were vacant. *What have they done to him?*

A vicious growl itched deep within, tempting me to take Sairen wolf form and find Korland. There was no human inside that monster. There couldn't be—his subtle, human-like features didn't convince me.

Fixing my eyes on Kiran, I noticed drool dripped from his

bottom lip. I snapped my fingers in front of his face.

"Come on…" I snapped again.

This time, Kiran blinked slowly, and his arm twitched just before color came back into his face. His eyebrows drew together while the corners of his mouth drooped.

Once Kiran noticed me, he vigorously shook his head and then leaned back in the chair.

"Who—" He struggled to get words out.

"It's me, Lorraine." I searched his eyes, but my name didn't seem to register. "Snowflake," I added with a hint of both desperation and disgust. "Kiran, please. You know me." I sniffed to soothe my own discomfort with the eerie silence. "There's no time for this," I whispered, glancing over at the door the avros had departed through, and the stairway to our escape.

A heavy darkness constricted my lungs. I tightened my jaw as I stared at him, waiting.

"Lorraine? Ah, yes, Lorraine," he whispered to himself. "The king…" Kiran rubbed his eyes and then stood. "I'm remembering."

My eyes flickered at his reference to 'the king,' but I smiled at his recollection.

"Welcome back," I beamed. Letting out a sigh of relief, I placed my hand on his shoulder and turned him around.

"I need you to go up those stairs and wait for me. Just keep quiet. I'm going to find Osouf."

How could I pull this off?

"Oh, wait, where is he? You know, don't you?" I asked.

Kiran took a step forward and then looked back at me wordlessly. His hair was a mess, strands of hair falling over the wrong side of his hairline. I let out an exasperated breath.

"Just go," I said, still uncertain what I was doing. Something had been done to Kiran. Why wasn't he telling me where to find Osouf?

Kiran nodded and leaped up the steps.

With a shaky hand, I opened the door, venturing further inside the prison. A long hallway was flanked by jail cells. The place reeked of rusted iron and wet wood. My nose burned, a sneeze building. One finally escaped me.

Noise filled the hall as the prisoners became aware of my presence. Many of them whistled and hollered, "Hey, over here," and "Come over here, young lady." They begged to be let out of their cells. *Would it be a good idea to free them? What had been done to them?*

But a humming stood out above their grimy voices. Focusing on the melody, I drowned out everything else and followed the tune until I found a young woman with black hair sitting with her legs crossed. Her narrow eyes looked me over from behind the bars of her cell. She stared back at the wall and continued her song.

"Shimmering silence gleam in the night.
Bring to me the red moonlight.
Serenity shine deep inside, the remedy for a great design.
Fallen wolves, fallen wolves, watch out for fallen wolves."

The girl finished her song, her eyes glimmering in the tiny light that came from an opening above. She didn't seem to care that I was still standing there, watching.

The lyrics of her song bounced around my brain as I tried to make sense of them. But then I got a whiff of something so strange and so intense that it made my tonsils sore.

In the next cell were two Sairen wolves. One was male, the other female. Both were in their human forms, watching me quietly. The scent of Sairen blood was mild in comparison to the pungent aroma of whatever else lingered in this place.

Cautiously, I leaned against the bars of their cell, looking for a way to release them. The woman flashed me a look. "I wouldn't do that if I were you."

"You don't want to be free?" I asked.

"Doesn't matter; you need to get out of here," the woman warned.

Why wouldn't it matter?

"It does matter. Don't worry, I'll get you out." As I pulled at the lock, her face contorted with anger. I backed off, searching her eyes. There were no signs of desire to leave, as if she accepted a horrid fate. Her cheeks sagged with exhaustion. Her skin, though an olive complexion, was pale, much like the young girl who was singing.

"How long have you been in here?" I probed.

The man standing next to her, who'd been chewing on a twig, suddenly grunted and reached for the iron bars. As he pushed his face between the bars, I stumbled back.

"Did you not hear her?" He pulled the stick from his mouth and threw it away. "Get out of here!"

Unable to free the Sairens, I raced to the nearest door. As I entered the other side, white walls flashed in contrast to the dark, cluttered space behind me. The wall to the left had a door with a petite glass window. Through the window, I glimpsed the top of someone's head—chocolate-brown hair, similar to mine.

I drew closer to the window, peering through it. My breath hitched and my mouth fell open. There he was! My brother sat with his back to the wall, hugging his knees. I tried the door, but it was locked. Repeatedly, I shook the door, pulling and pushing…but it wouldn't budge. I took several steps back and then slammed my body into the door. It was no use; all I did was bruise my side.

Footsteps echoed from the other side of the door at the end of the hallway. Placing my hand over the glass of Osouf's door, I whispered, "I'll come back for you. I promise." My eyes stung. I was leaving with a stranger rather than my own brother.

It wasn't how this was supposed to go.

Osouf lifted his head. The bags under his eyes were dark purple. He was thinner than when I had seen him last. His eyes glistened as he saw me. For a moment, I thought I could lead him out of there along with Kiran, but then the chains around his wrists caught my eye.

At the sound of more footsteps, Osouf looked around. They were just outside the far door of the corridor I occupied. Two voices spoke; the doorknob turned, but the door didn't open. The sound was muffled, but one particular voice made the hairs on my back stand on end—Korland.

My heart stalled as I stumbled backwards. I couldn't look away from Osouf, even as I reached for the door I'd just come through. But he vigorously shooed me away. "Get out of here," he mouthed.

As I opened the door and slid behind it, the other swung wide. I'd barely caught glimpse of Korland and another avro. Pain stabbed at my lungs as I sprinted past all the prison cells and into the room where I had found Kiran. Taking the stairs three steps at a time, I leaped up them and opened the trapdoor, then crawled through it. Catching my breath, I rested my hands on my knees.

Kiran's wide smile startled me as I straightened. It took everything I had not to burst into tears. But the possibility of Korland being right behind us forced me to focus.

"We need to fly out," I stated. Kiran gave a blank stare. "Are you able to transform?"

"Not at the moment…I don't think." Like a shy child, he held his arm with the other, staring at the ground.

A groan rattled behind my teeth as I glanced at the trapdoor. "Fine," I said. "Just ride on my back, then."

After I took Sairen wolf form, Kiran clumsily climbed on my back. His weight rested at the end of my shoulder blades. All four of my legs wobbled for a moment before I readjusted myself.

Spreading my wings, I backed up to the edge of the roof and sprinted to the other side. As I reached the ledge, I flapped my wings and leaped into the air.

It was risky to fly out, and with Kiran's weight, I wasn't sure I could make it that far. Nevertheless, we made it just far enough away from the prison, landing in the forest. After catching my breath, we were able to run lightly toward the cabin and I didn't think we'd been followed.

The sun had set by the time we made it back. A wave of relief washed over me as I shifted back to two legs and gazed over the place we called home. *We made it.* Somehow, I'd managed to make it out of the Alcazar and successfully rescue Kiran.

Of course, there was Osouf—his sagging features were engraved in my mind—but I had found him. He was alive. There was no longer any doubt in my mind; I would get him out of there.

A peaceful sigh flowed from my chest as we walked inside Alden's cabin. The only person awake to greet us was Cylus. He flashed a scornful look when he noticed Kiran following behind me.

"I would ask where you've been, but that answers my question," he commented, nodding at Kiran. "Besides, Luke filled me in, except…he said you were going to rescue Osouf. I didn't believe that. We were beginning to get worried, but I insisted everyone get some rest and that I'd go looking for you if you didn't return." Cylus leaned back in his chair, sipping from a glass of iced water.

"I tr—"

"Spare me the details," Cylus interrupted, raising his palm. My mouth was still open, ready to speak, but then I felt Kiran's breath on my neck.

As I turned to face him, I saw the same blank stare from when I first found him. Kiran scratched the back of his head, eyes wandering. I shoved him towards the hallway. "You really need some rest. Go to bed," I urged him.

Those bright-green eyes of his seemed dimmer than I recalled. What in Elohi had they done to him in the short time before I rescued him?

Kiran managed a few steps forward before he turned around, as if looking for confirmation on where to go.

"Oh, I forgot you've been sleeping on the couch."

Kiran shrugged and stared off into the distance. Cylus suggested Kiran sleep in Luke's room tonight. I blinked at Cylus, waiting for a smart remark, or some sort of reprimand. It was odd to see him being kind to Kiran.

After I pointed Kiran down the hall, I cocked my head at Cylus and crossed my arms. *What was that about?*

Once the door was shut, Cylus set down his glass of water and leaned forward, hands clasped. His mind seemed elsewhere; his eyes were wide and his face flushed.

"You look like you've seen a ghost," I said. "And what happened with Luke? How's his wound?"

Cylus's chest rose, his eyes flickered, and for a moment, I anticipated the usual disapproving response to my teasing—a hint of anger and reproach. But instead, Cylus rubbed his hands over his head.

"I feel like I have," he said. "When you left…" He paused and exhaled. "Which I noticed, by the way. You aren't so sneaky." Cylus took another sip of his water before continuing. "We saw him." Those dark eyes of his had never seemed so bright. "The king."

"The…what?" I had thought he was mocking me for sneaking off to rescue Kiran. But there was something different in his tone.

"King Ezrai," he said, emphasizing the word "king." Cylus bounced out of his seat and drew closer. "This is not a joke, Lorraine. He's real. And Luke is well; Ezrai healed him."

My lips parted. My mind was blank. Drawing in a sharp breath, I scanned Cylus's face. His expression was one of awe and delight. Still, I couldn't find words. Alden had told us about the king but Cylus and I both had our doubts.

Mulling over the information, I concluded that Cylus must have seen something, or *someone,* and I needed to know more. "So, what was he like?"

Calmer now, he fell back into his chair and invited me to take a seat across from him. He looked distant, licking his dry lips.

"Well, he's…" Cylus rubbed his chin. "He's like us, but more like you." He mumbled inaudibly to himself and then cleared his throat. "You know, a white wolf. Except bigger, brighter, and there's this…" His voice trailed off. He just sat there, staring off into space.

I raised a brow at him. Of all of us, he had always been the most composed, other than his ruthless outbursts directed at me. But I had never seen Cylus so amazed and speechless.

"Alright. Good to know. So, what else?" I shrugged.

"You must see him in person. I'm not sure my descriptions do him justice."

"I'd say not."

He covered one hand with the other, his dark cheeks glowing. A warm, tingling sensation spread in my chest as I studied him. My heart slowed in the serenity that surrounded us. *What is this feeling?*

Hope. The kind of hope that would make one believe anything was possible. Yet, as quickly as it came, it was gone. My skin chilled and I shook off the feeling. It was a fragile flame that went out at the tiniest puff of breath.

Standing, I paced between the kitchen and the den area where Cylus remained seated. *The king is…real? Where has he been all this time?*

Suddenly, I found myself not wanting to hear anything else about the *king*. But Cylus continued. "The thing about King Ezrai is, he can Spark, like—" He gestured to me but then quickly retrieved his hand. "Well, like most white Sairen wolves. Except his power is different."

I leaned in.

"His power heals them."

The tingling sensation intensified. "The avros," I mumbled to myself, but Cylus heard me.

"Yes. They return to human form. Restored. I assume that's the way Kiran was healed."

Now facing him, I searched his eyes, waiting for him to say it.

"All the avros locked in the barn are human now. And all the others sleeping on the ground from Robin's bolts, also human."

I thought about Robin's cousin. She must be celebrating. I grinned as I visualized her victory—our victory. I imagined Osouf returning home, and fighting by his side again.

For some time I daydreamed about that day—being reunited with my brother. Cylus stared out the window, subdued.

"Is that everything? You seem exhausted," I said.

"There is one more thing." Cylus's eyes never strayed from the window. "It would seem Shariee has a gift we did not know about. She didn't know herself."

"What's that?"

"She's a Shilo, like Kiran."

His words brought me back to that evening we had first met Kiran. *No wonder she wasn't fully affected by the shadows.*

Cylus stood, wordlessly announcing that he was done for the night.

With nothing left to say, I went to the bed that Shariee and I shared and drifted off to sleep.

Tossing and turning as I tried to get to sleep, pieces of the day's events played out in front of me. The Avros, running to the barn and climbing out of it, seeing Osouf. The dark circles under his eyes made me shudder.

Pushing away the image, I imagined King Ezrai. I visualized a large white Sairen wolf, but that's all I could make out because he was blurry. I rubbed my eyes, blinking. As the king became clearer, something changed. The wolf before me was like a spirit and fiery red. A loud thumping noise sounded, and I jolted awake.

My chest heaved as I sat up in bed. Shariee groaned and pulled the covers closer to her face as she turned away from me. I slowly breathed in through my nostrils and then out my mouth.

A subtle light glowed outside the window. Unable to fall back asleep anyway, I rolled out of bed, stretching as I stood up, and dragged my feet over to pull back the curtains. A bluish-grey color highlighted the horizon.

I squinted through the dusty glass. A white blob took shape as it moved closer to the window, towards me. As the shape became clearer, I realized that it was a white Sairen wolf.

Could it be the king?

"No," I whispered to myself. "It couldn't be." I slid out the bedroom door, down the hallway, and tiptoed out of the cabin, barefoot in my human form.

Once I had spotted him, there was a long pause. Bright-brown eyes gazed at me without blinking. Just as I was about to greet him, a light breeze blew, carrying his scent in my direction. Something about him was familiar, but I couldn't quite place it. The Sairen sat down and curled his tail around his front paws. My eyes widened as the white Sairen wolf tilted his head in a taunting manner. It wasn't the king…

I stood there, mouth gaping.

The way she tilted her head, *that scent…*

It was Robin.

17

Robin transformed to human shape, crossing her arms with a grin. "Surprised?"

"Thought you were someone else. I never imagined seeing you as a Sairen wolf, though."

"I'm only here because you all clearly need my help," she sneered.

Pressing my lips together, I glared at her. "I take it you're here to join our pack?"

"That's the idea," she said.

"Come inside," I breathed, gesturing for her to follow me inside the cabin. *I must know how...*

A few days had passed since Kiran's rescue. Although the pack and I tried many times to ask him what happened before I found him and why Korland had wanted him, he refused to talk about it. Eventually, I gave up. He didn't want to tell us, and my thoughts were fixed on my brother—those dark rims around his eyes haunted me each passing hour.

The hope I had felt when I thought of King Ezrai and how he healed those who had turned came and went. If what Cylus had witnessed was true, Arah and Korland would be no match for this king of ours.

At other times, I became conflicted. Where was Ezrai now? And why could he not just bust down those prison walls and rescue Osouf and everyone else inside? But Cylus had repeated to me multiple times now: "It's not that simple." Alden concurred with Cylus, using his customary cryptic phrases.

Nothing made sense. The more they tried to justify the king, the more angry I felt. Everyone was so driven and their eyes glistened any time I brought up Ezrai—as if they had seen something magical. Yet, as mighty as they described him to be, avros were still roaming Elohi. Humans continued to be turned into them as they became part of the darkness invading the world. My brother and others were bound in our enemy's prison.

My doubts grew. Though I knew Cylus wouldn't have lied, I still wondered. Nevertheless, the way he described what had happened, that new sparkle in his eye…it was believable. Then I'd seen Robin as a white Sairen wolf. She claimed Ezrai had transformed her into one of us.

That night Robin showed up as a Sairen, she had confirmed that her cousin, Raven, was human again. Along with Robin's father and uncle, Raven was helping them defend Hyra.

Having never seen such a heavy attack by avros, the pack that had assisted us stayed within our region. Apparently, Alden howled the melodic Sairen tune to communicate we needed help before he joined us in the fight.

There was talk of them joining us to infiltrate Korland's prison.

Yet still, the pack believed Kiran's initial assertion that we needed a white wolf to Spark, so they insisted Robin train with me.

I pleaded multiple times that we go rescue Osouf now. After all, I had been successful in retrieving Kiran, alone—without Sparking. But Kiran said by now they'd have noticed him missing and increased their guard. Alden also warned us of acting prematurely. Ultimately, it was my respect for the old Sairen that kept me from barging back in myself. Every once in a while, I would ponder the notion of convincing Robin to accompany me in getting my brother back, but then other times, I feared she'd tell the others of my plan. She might think of my plan as unwise. In a way, she'd be right.

They couldn't understand how Osouf wouldn't leave my mind—his thin face and sunken eyes. He was the only family I had left and there was no unseeing him in that condition. The Alcazar drew me, like a moth to a flame. If I could just go back there and…

I uncurled my fists when the newest member of the pack nudged me. "You good?" Robin asked sincerely.

"Oh. Yeah," I muttered, dropping my arm. I'd almost forgotten we were waiting on Dasan for training.

"Great. Ready for me to show you up?" Robin snickered as she stretched in preparation.

"I'd like to see you try," I teased half-heartedly. Everyone knew of my difficulty Sparking, but Robin standing next to me as a Sairen wolf with the potential to Spark had me determined. Her condescending hand on her hip made my blood boil.

I couldn't get used to seeing her as a Sairen wolf. Not just because she was human before, but because of my first encounter with her. She distrusted any creature that was non-human, and couldn't stand that magical creatures had entered Elohi. Even if it meant that protectors such as Sairen wolves had come to save the humans. Her arrogance annoyed me, though her dislike of

Sairens made her becoming one of us all the more amusing.

Robin had good reason, though, to accept king Ezrai's gift. Having believed that her cousin could be saved and then seeing that become a reality, Robin couldn't turn down Ezrai's offer. Not when Ezrai promised her the ability to change others back to human form the way he could—he'd teach her in due time. I knew a struggle still resided in her, though.

As Dasan approached, Robin turned to me with a shaky breath. "So, how exactly does this training work?" Her tone sounded eager.

I tittered to myself. Robin looked puzzled.

Dasan gave us curt nod in greeting. "Lorraine. Robin."

We acknowledged him in return by saying his name in unison. Dasan's eyes lit up. "Ah. Perfect. You two have similar energy." The trainer placed his pointer finger over his mouth, as if pleased with his subjects. "Quite good."

"What?" Robin mouthed to me. But all I could do was barely refrain from laughing. She really had no idea what she had gotten herself into. "He doesn't act like a father who has lost his daughter," she mumbled, just barely audible for me to hear. I nodded.

In human form, Dasan sat down on the grass, closed his eyes, and pressed his palms against the ground. To my surprise, Robin mimicked him, eyes closed. I followed suit, placing my hand just above the ground.

"Robin. Do tell me, who are you?" Dasan inquired.

My eyes flew open. He'd never spoken during this portion of my training. Without hesitation, the Sairen wolf next to me stuck out her chest and lifted her chin.

"Robin Jelani. Daughter of Falcon and Kambri Jelani," she stated.

"Yes. Robin Jelani, daughter of Falcon and Kambri Jelani," Dasan repeated. "What else?"

"I was human, until I met Ezrai."

"I'd say you are so much more. Enlighten us: who are you now?"

With her eyes still shut, Robin began to dig deeper. "I'm a part of Ezrai's army now. Neriah's light flows through me. A white wolf. Strong, unmatched wits, capable of Sparking," she claimed.

I glared at her as Robin grinned. Her chest rose and fell while her skin glowed bronze.

Robin's brow twitched and her lips parted. She lifted her head higher, as if to soak in the sun's rays. The tiny hairs along my arms stood on end.

Holding my breath, I gaped at her hovering hand. A blue-and-white spark flickered beneath her fingers. Robin jolted back and her eyes flew open.

"I felt it!" she gushed.

Unphased, Dasan stood up and brushed himself off. "Excellent, time for transformation."

I remained seated in the grass as both Dasan and Robin walked past me. Letting out an exasperated sigh, I rested my cheek over my fist. As they proceeded with Robin's training, I attempted to ease the tension in my neck. My fingers moved in circles, applying pressure to that one spot that pulled at my nerves.

"I believe you are ready," the instructor said to Robin.

Glancing up at them, I found the two staring at me. Dasan motioned for me to come over with that crazed look in his eyes.

"Lorraine, you know the drill. I suppose I'll allow you the honors. Something tells me it would be better that way, yes?" A wide smirk grew from cheek to cheek.

Without saying a word, I nodded and strode to the edge of the cliff, planting myself beside Robin.

"He'd like for me to show you something." I placed my arm around her and pulled her closer.

Robin squirmed out of my grip, sliding her foot along the

cliffside. She twisted her body around. Quickly, she rebalanced, keeping herself from falling. "What in Elohi is going on here?" she cursed under her breath.

I paused, remembering this portion of my training. The memory of my heart thumping in my chest, my brain freezing just before I hit the ground...

Dasan is insane. Could I really push her off the edge like that?

Robin crossed her arms with her head slightly bent, glaring up at me. The expression was the same one she'd given me at the market, the first time we met and she twisted my arm behind my back.

Taking a step closer, she watched me intently. One thing I knew for sure: Robin would be fine. But payback for the day we first met was long overdue.

"I'll give you the warning I was never given. Fly," I whispered just before shoving her off the cliff.

I turned my back and walked away from the cliffside, hearing her echoed scream. I drew in a deep breath and waited. Dasan sat down, cross-legged, picking at the loose skin around his nails. *How can he be so calm right now?*

What felt like several minutes passed by. Robin was nowhere in sight. I looked over to Dasan for reassurance, but he stood with his arms behind his back, whistling.

I looked at the place I had pushed her. I imagined marching right up to our trainer and teaching him a lesson.

A rustling nearby distracted me. As I turned to the forest, Kiran stepped out from between the trees—his eyes darted between Dasan and me. But before either of us could acknowledge him, a flow of static tickled my back. I whirled around to see Robin, in Sairen wolf form, flashes of blue and white surrounding her.

"Marvelous!" Dasan shouted, clapping. Kiran joined in, clapping too, though with an odd, blank stare. I summoned a thin smile and applauded myself. Robin hadn't only Sparked, but she was still holding onto the power, letting it flow and zap around her.

With flushed cheeks, I watched everyone's amusement grow the longer she held onto her newfound power. I felt certain that I would never fully Spark. How could it be this simple, this easy to control?

I shook my head and put my hands together more enthusiastically. If I couldn't Spark, or if the king was too busy to help us, Robin was now my ticket to rescuing Osouf. A warmth rolled up my back and spread throughout my body. I found myself pulled in the direction of the prison.

I'll go. I must go.

"Shall we work on you next?" Dasan asked.

"No," I said, a little too quickly. "I'm not really feeling up to it now, but it's fine. If Robin can Spark, we can proceed with the plan. We don't need to waste time on me."

"Alright, then, let us head back to Alden's," Dasan responded.

I wasn't particularly thrilled about having to train later; however, there was a newfound bit of hope. I snickered to myself knowing Robin would certainly have the guts to go on my daring adventure. Which was important, because Kiran was still recovering. Whatever they'd done to him, his memory had become fuzzy. That didn't matter anymore, though; I had been to Korland's prison and found Osouf myself.

As we arrived back at the cabin, Kiran and Robin went inside while Dasan held out his arm, keeping me from joining them. "Let us have a chat, shall we?"

We stayed on the porch, sitting on some old wooden chairs. Dasan ran his hand through his dark curls, while lifting his leg so that his foot could rest over his knee. "Alright, then. Let me have it," he said.

"I'm not mad at you." Though there was a hint of frustration in my tone, it was a personal issue.

"I never suggested you were mad at me." The instructor leaned forward, rubbing his mustache. "You would like to know why your peer made further progress than you, yes?"

"A lot of questions come to mind, actually."

"Ah. Yes." With a blank expression, Dasan twirled the end of his mustache between his finger and his thumb. "I've been training your breed for quite some time now. Learning to Spark is a mixture of connection and the right amount of fear in the right place."

"Connection?" I questioned.

"A connection to the Light and yourself, confidence. You struggle, Lorraine, because you do not know who you are." Dasan put his hands together and sighed. My failure seemed to bother him. "I'm exquisite at reading minds, wouldn't you say?" He threw his head back, cackling. He was mad—clearly a lunatic.

"Or you're just psychotic," I mocked with contemptuous laughter. "And why didn't you tell me this before?"

"Everything is about timing, my friend." His amusement faded and his stare became serious. "There is a battle brewing inside of you," he claimed. "If you want to Spark, you must find yourself first. Ask yourself, 'Who am I?'"

Who am I?

"You're starting to sound like Alden." I glared at him. Deciphering Alden's riddles was never fun; his words would crawl under my skin the way Dasan's were now—tiresome. "How is this constructive? How are you this enthusiastic when your daughter is lost and going through who knows what right now?"

His eyes clouded as his goofy grin disappeared. "I can only do so much. Sitting around and sulking will not get me anywhere," he said.

Dasan stood up and turned his back to me as he looked off to my left, hands clasped behind him. "May I offer this piece of advice…be slow to anger. It's a nasty beast."

18

A LIGHTER ATMOSPHERE FILLED ALDEN'S HOME. THINGS SEEMED TO have turned around with King Ezrai making an appearance and the pack gaining another white wolf with Sparking capabilities. As word got out that the king had joined us, Sairen wolves and humans across Elohi would be filled with hope.

But hope had always felt like a dangerous thing to me. This was not the time to let our guard down, or forget about those who'd been captured. The memory of Osouf made me restless. There was talk of us putting our previous plan into action, but Kiran intervened.

"It's not enough," he snapped. "We'll need more."

Cylus cocked his head at Kiran with a menacing glare. "Watch your tone," Cylus demanded, then glanced over at me briefly. "Lorraine has waited long enough. Was it not your plan to rescue her brother?" Lowering his voice, he inched himself closer to the green-eyed Sairen. "Lorraine managed to sneak into this secure prison you speak of, pulled you out, and brought you here…without Sparking. Yet, there is one among us who can Spark now. Why the sudden hesitation?"

Kiran swallowed. His eyes bounced around the room. "Because I know Korland—"

"Of course you do," Cylus interjected.

Kiran's eyes narrowed at him, but he quickly returned to his previous train of thought. "Korland will have the prison more heavily guarded now, which means more Shadow Sairens. One Sairen who can Spark is not enough now."

Alden opened his mouth to speak, but paused to enjoy the aroma of his coffee. After taking a sip, he looked over at Kiran and Cylus.

"By now, Korland would have noticed you're missing," Alden reasoned. "I'd imagine he's taking someone sneaking into his prison more seriously. He won't let it happen again so easily. But there's something I'm having a troubling time understanding."

"What's that?" Kiran asked defensively.

Alden gulped down his coffee before answering. "Why he let you leave in the first place."

Kiran slumped in his seat with a thumb pressed against his chin. The room grew still. All eyes were on Kiran now.

"I was under the impression that I was rescued," he retorted, without so much as a peek in my direction. His voice was cold and distant.

"Perhaps," Alden said. Looking away, he redirected everyone's focus to the previous debate. "I do believe Kiran is right. There is no way to know what their security arrangements will be like now. We need further assistance."

"How about the *king?*" Kiran spoke of Ezrai with disdain.

Those bright-green eyes of his were only met with desolate stares. A bit perplexed, he continued, "This would be a small task for him, right?"

Everyone leaned in; even Luke remained quiet and still. Cylus clicked his tongue against the roof of his mouth.

"Do you not think the king has better things to do?" I shifted against the sofa cushions as Cylus continued. "It is not to say that Osouf isn't important, of course, but we are at war with evil, and Ezrai is our key to winning this war. Why would we put him in harm's way for the one when that would risk his mission to save the world?"

I mulled over Cylus's words. Though I still couldn't imagine this king, it was evident by everyone's reports that someone named Ezrai existed, and he was extremely powerful. That much seemed true.

"You're forgetting that Osouf was born under a blood moon, Cylus," I said.

"No, I haven't forgotten. Many have been born during a blood moon, for all we know, the one from Talli's dream hasn't even been born yet, or was born and already killed...or, perhaps it is the king himself."

Ignoring Cylus and me, Kiran spoke up. "My apologies." Kiran coughed. "What I knew of him must be wrong, because I thought he was powerful and that he cared about the one as much as the many."

"What exactly is your goal here?" Cylus growled. "Forget it. Of course, the king has great power; whether or not he'll take on this small mission is the issue."

"I believe he would," Alden intervened. "But we should proceed with caution. I myself have little understanding of the power of the stone Korland possesses."

The more we discussed Osouf's rescue with little progression, the heavier my breaths became.

"I know a way we could find out more," Robin spoke up. "My cousin was an avro. She may have some information about the prison."

Fidgeting with my hands, I thought over the situation. Was it true that Ezrai cared for us so much that he would go out of his way to save just one person? I couldn't imagine such a thing, though the idea filled me with hope. But what kept Ezrai from going to the Alcazar now?

THE WHOLE PACK WAITED IN THE DEN WHILE ROBIN WENT TO visit Raven to see if she knew anything about the prison.

"I'm bored," Luke announced. Though in the middle of braiding her hair, Shariee gave her younger brother a swift kick to the shin.

"What? What did I say wrong this time?" he asked.

"Sorry, but now is not the time to be complaining, buddy. This is important; we're waiting on Robin. You're just gonna have to wait with us."

Several more minutes passed by before I sensed Robin was near.

The other Sairens all exhaled as Robin approached the front door, but she didn't open it. Two voices mumbled beyond the door. Someone else was out there with Robin.

Luke tiptoed past us and pressed his ear to the door. The rest of us gathered behind him. I made eye contact with Cylus, who

130

only shrugged in response. Normally, he'd be the first to force Luke to behave; however, he too seemed curious. Alden remained in his chair, leaving us be.

"Man, if she says 'mhmm' one more time." Luke pantomimed fake punches at the door. Shariee placed her finger over her lips, urging her brother to be silent. Not that it mattered; Robin knew we were waiting.

"Well, anything?" I asked after a few minutes.

Luke moved his head away from the door. "Not really. Something about gathering a few of us and going somewhere."

"You'd make a terrible spy," Cylus teased.

Robin swung open the door and all of us froze. Noticing us close by, she raised a brow. "Alright, listen up," she began. "Raven has learned some valuable information from her time as an avro. We think it'd be best if a few of you came to hear it."

Beside her was Dasan. His gaze appeared distant. *When did he get here?*

"Dasan," Alden greeted my trainer. "What brings you here?"

Slowly, Dasan turned to the elder Sairen. "Fate, it would seem. Or so I hope."

"I found him on my way back here; Raven may know where they've moved his daughter," Robin added.

"I'd like to go," Kiran blurted, but Cylus placed his arm out in front of him and stepped forward.

"Back it up, boy," Cylus said. "I don't think you're fully recovered just yet."

"He's right—we can share whatever information we learn when we get back," Alden interjected, rocking in his chair. The elder Sairen wolf gave a gentle smile as he grabbed his cane, which leaned against the wall beside him. "I'm going."

"Of course, Alden should be there," Cylus agreed, walking to the door.

"Okay, look…all of you could come for all I care, but Dad's

house is small. Not to mention Raven is traumatized by her time as an avro. Though she's agreed to answer any questions and give us information, let's not crowd her." Robin let out an exasperated sigh. "Alright, Alden, Cylus, Lorraine…Dasan. Let's go."

"Oh, I'm going, I'm going," Alden said.

"Right. Let's get going." Robin was the first out the door, leading the way for the three of us while Kiran, Shariee, and Luke stayed behind.

When we arrived at Robin's house in the village, Robin's dad greeted us with a sturdy handshake. "Hey there, I'm Falcon, but people call me Falco. Raven is pouring tea. Please, come inside and have a seat." We crowded inside. With a wide grin, Falco motioned for us to seat ourselves at the dining table. Another man stood beside him, solidly built but not quite as brawny as Falco, though they had the same nose.

"Seeing as how my brother here left me out, I'm Finch," he chimed in, extending his hand to shake ours. "Oh, and the people around here call me…well, Finch," he mocked. Robin's uncle chortled, holding his belly as it bounced.

"Yeah, yeah." Falco placed his elbow on the table and rested his head in his hand. "Ignore him. We've never had wolves as guests before." He locked gazes with Robin. "But now that my daughter is one of you, you're family."

"Hello. Tea, anyone?" A woman about Robin's age shuffled into the room from around the corner, careful not to spill the two cups of piping hot liquid in her hands. I recognized her—the shape of her face, the fierce stare…she was the avro I had almost killed.

Robin's cousin had darker hair and eyes. Her voice was raspy and yet bold. Raven worked her way around the table, bringing out cup after cup, presumably from the kitchen, then setting them down in front of us. She truly fit her name—Raven. Her dark skin shone.

The coils of her hair remained perfectly intact as Raven joined us at the table. Holding her hands together, she leaned forward. A determined expression came down over her features.

"This is how this *teatime* is going to go," Raven said abruptly. "I have the floor, and you will not interrupt me. You can ask questions when I say 'do you have any questions?' but we are not here for fellowship, to have a good time, or to get to know one another."

"Raven," said Finch in a warning tone.

"The tea was my idea," Robin said with an awkward grin.

Robin's cousin straightened, somewhat calmer now. "You are here because we have a common enemy. I have information and I will provide said information if it helps save the human race. Do we understand each other?" Raven's jaw clenched, her lips pressing together as she folded her arms.

"Sounds fair," Cylus answered.

The arch in her brow disappeared. "I like you," she declared, smiling for the first time since we had met her in human form.

Her gaze scanned the room till it landed on me. For a moment, I stared back at those dark, piercing eyes. I remembered them plainly, from the face of the avro that I almost killed. She was human now. I searched for words, but none came.

Glancing down offered no escape from the spewing hatred in her next words. "I especially don't want to hear a disruption from you."

"Raven, I—"

Her fist slammed the table as she stood, her finger pointed at me.

"Keep my name from your lips," she spat. "You nearly killed me. I saw it. I saw it in your eyes! You could have killed me without a thought. Bet you were there when my mother was killed." Her voice became shaky as her eyes watered. "You're a monster."

"Raven," Finch said. "Breathe." Her dad demonstrated a

breathing technique for her to mimic. Thankfully, it worked, but it didn't stop the tears from falling down her cheeks. Robin reached over and held Raven's hand.

"M-my mother was killed too," I stammered. "And my father. Or at least, I think." The silence in the room made my heart sink. What good would it do to tell her of my pain? But she had to know—to know what we Sairens had sacrificed fighting for Elohi.

My lip began to quiver. "My brother is being held hostage in Korland's prison." Hunched over now, I searched the ground for something, anything to focus on other than Robin's cousin and her pain—and my own. "Raven, I'm sorry," I whispered.

Falco cleared his throat. "The avros who have turned back to human form all deal with some sort of trauma as a result of the evil they committed." He glanced at his niece. "Each one has a different path to recovery. As you can see, we're working on anger management."

"Forgiveness," Alden corrected. "The most difficult task of bravery." Wrinkles framed the old man's expression. "And you are a brave one, I can sense that."

"She is," Finch chimed in. "My girl came back to us, and even helped others in her position. She's strong. Beautiful. Resilient."

"Like the flock of birds…" Robin mumbled.

"We fly together," Raven finished, grinning as she wiped away her tears. The Jelanis all raised their arms in a diagonal position at chest level and hand curled into a fist. Alden, Cylus and I remained quiet.

I didn't know much of Alden's past, I knew none of Dasan's, and Cylus never spoke much of his, but this was the closest I could remember being to a group of humans.

Their family dynamic stirred a deep longing in me. This was the sort of bond I'd been missing for over a month. A dark-grey hue filled the windows as storm clouds gathered in the distance.

"This war is a nasty one," said Cylus. "We do what we must,

Raven. I hope you may come to understand that. The right path is not always so simple. In a perfect world, maybe, but you know more than most that it isn't perfect. We fight, we protect, we save humans the best way we know how. You have a choice. A powerful one. If we work together, we can do better. Maybe save others like yourself."

"Tell us what you invited us here for." Robin placed her arm around her cousin.

"I'll start," Falco suggested. He began by recounting what had happened in the village after we left—the golden electricity that flowed through each avro still alive, restoring them to their human state.

Then he related finding Raven, now in human form, and how he had directed capable people to tend to the revived. Over the next few days, Falco, his brother, Raven, and many others came to learn what the transformed people had seen and heard while they were avros.

As Falco spoke, Raven looked like she'd been transported back in time. But when Falco mentioned Korland's stone, her eyes brightened.

"The red stone." Raven stared past us. "That's right. The one that is in Kor's staff."

"Korland?"

Robin's cousin glared at me. "Yes, *Kor*," she hissed.

"They say it's not from here," Finch informed us. "As in, not of this world."

To my surprise, Alden spoke up. "That's because it's not." The old man lifted his head, the worn skin around his hands wrinkling as he clasped his fingers. "And it doesn't belong to him, not even to Arah."

"That's right," Raven said matter-of-factly. "I heard the stone is connected to *Ezrai somehow.*"

CYLUS AND I EXCHANGED A LOOK. ALDEN KEPT MUCH FROM US, and we never understood why, but it was evident he held secrets.

"Here's the thing," Raven said. "I believe the stone is what they call the Ruach. Up close, that thing looks more like a crystal."

"Wait," I blurted, but Raven tilted her head at me with a threatening expression.

Right, no interruptions.

I sank deeper into my chair. Avoiding eye contact with Raven, I bit my lip. Only when she returned to the subject did my shoulders loosen.

"Here's the thing. There is only one Ruach, and it belongs to the Light. Arah stole it, I believe, over a hundred years ago. There's suspicion that the Ruach is giving him pushback and that Arah is having a hard time wielding its power. Anyway, he's handed it off to Kor to do his dirty work. As prideful as he is, Arah is afraid to face Ezrai himself while Ezrai's power is intact." She searched the room. The wind stirred unruly bush branches to tap the window.

"All I know is, Arah somehow discovered that the Ruach is drawn to Sairens born under a blood moon. Though I don't know how he came to the conclusion, from there he discovered the blood of a Sairen wolf born under a red moon can draw out Ezrai's power." Her gaze turned to me as thunder rumbled in the distance. "Which he already has."

"Osouf." The name escaped my lips in a whisper.

Unperturbed, Raven went on. "And, if I'm not mistaken, the phrase was 'spirit of fire.' When I was a monster…" She winced. "At first, we kept hearing about the red wolf prophecy, and Arah bragged about having wiped out almost all Sairens born under a red moon. Then he learned he needed the blood of one to extract the king's powers. But there's a piece I'm missing; they were careful not to tell us everything. Either way, we can't let Arah gain ultimate authority. Humanity will all become avros or some sort of mindless monsters ruled by Arah." She quieted, lost in some sort of trance.

Robin patted Raven's shoulder. Both Falco and Finch watched her with caution in their expressions. I thought back to what Finch said before—how Raven was traumatized and still battling the darkness. Of course, I didn't know what it was like to become an avro, to give into the darkness and then be brought back to the light. But the poison of the Shadow Sairens had given me a taste of that.

I shuddered.

"I will not allow this to happen," Raven assured us. "You three are now my closest allies. Like it or not, we're working together."

"What's not to like?" Alden remarked. Dasan nudged him, even my trainer, who was a bit eccentric himself, knew better than to respond with sarcasm.

Raven didn't share in Alden's humor. "I'm not talking about *your* pleasantries, it may not bother you." She placed her hand on her chest. "But it does me. To many of the world, you are no better than the avros. Though I'll admit, you are trying to protect us, and if it weren't for having met king Ezrai myself, I'd still be holding on to the belief that Sairens are evil too."

My hand moved to my mouth, covering up my amusement.

"Alright. Questions?" Raven asked.

Dasan raised his hand. Once Raven acknowledged him with a raised brow, he cleared his throat. "About my daughter, Ella…"

"Right. The redhead," she responded. "She's now in Arah's custody."

Dasan's jaw dropped and his eyes widened as he looked past her. "Oh no, Ella," he whispered to himself. "Why? What does that fool want with her?" Dasan's leg bounced beneath him as he looked at Raven. "What will happen to her?"

Raven leaned closer, unflinching. "Do you think I have a clue?" She pulled back. "You need to speak with Keone. He was also an avro before…he's one of the avros who transferred your daughter to Arah. All I know is, Arah needed her for something, and I don't know what."

Dasan's eyes scanned the room, unseeing. "Well alright then, carry on. But please do share with me later how I can find this Keone."

"Any other questions?" Raven asked.

The Jelani brothers studied us, but we remained quiet. My thoughts grew muddled with the new information. I contemplated Kiran's suggestion that Ezrai help us rescue Osouf. I held my breath. Osouf was the only known Sairen wolf currently alive that was born under a blood moon, which meant getting my brother back was an important mission with implications for the entire world.

As if she read my mind, Robin straightened, letting go of

Raven's hand and turning to face her cousin. "How exactly does it work? The blood of the red wolf can extract the stone's powers?"

"We don't know for sure. I'm not so sure Kor himself understands it." Raven slouched forward. "All I know is, the staff Korland carries has it's own powerful force that does not come from the Ruach. I would guess Arah has a magic of his own, that's the only way he can conjure up more evil weapons." She exhaled, shoulders sinking. "He's limited, of course, without Ezrai's magic. We suspect they can't fully see into the stone and that Arah is having trouble forcing it to reveal any secrets."

"I suggest we leave Ezrai out of our plans to rescue Osouf," Alden said. "It's too risky. In fact, Lorraine, it may be best if you stayed behind as well. Dasan mentioned your emotions are heightened at present."

"Wha—but I know the path," I argued. "I was able to get in myself."

Cylus curled his fingers into a ball, nostrils flaring. "How many times do we have to ask you not to be foolish?" he chided. "Kiran knows his way around too, remember? If you were the red wolf, we'd be in great trouble," he mumbled under his breath.

"Lucky for you I can't Spark," I retorted, "or I'd zap you."

"That's not...how Sparking works." Robin dropped her head into her palm. "It's difficult to explain, but it's not *really* electric, though it does behave a bit like it."

"I know," I said. "I've felt it. But Cylus doesn't know that."

"If I may," Finch intervened. "If all Korland needed to steal Ezrai's powers was Osouf's blood, why keep him alive?"

The pitter-patter of the rain outside filled the silence while Raven appeared to ponder Finch's question. I scooted to the edge of my chair, hoping she knew the answer.

"That, I am not sure of," she said.

Usually, the sounds of a summer storm would calm me like a

lullaby—the deep bass of thunder; the melodical voices of raindrops harmonizing as they tapped against different objects. But this time, I remained on edge.

Falco rubbed his chin. "Something isn't right. As wonderful it is that your brother is alive, Lorraine, there must be a reason why they haven't killed him yet. There's something we're missing. I don't like this."

"Nor do I," Alden agreed.

Raven fidgeted with her fingers, digging her nails into her palms. Her father snapped his fingers in front of her face and she came back to herself with a deep breath. Falco stood, inviting the rest of us to join him. "I think it best we give Raven some space now. Anyway, that's all the information we have for you."

Robin's dad stretched his arms behind his head and let out a ferocious yawn. We scurried out the door and returned to Alden's cabin.

Alden and Cylus told the others what we had learned. I sat still, staring off into nothingness. It wasn't until Alden was telling them about Ezrai's stone and the reason for Osouf's capture that reality sank in—we needed Ezrai, yet we also needed to protect him.

Lying back on the couch, I kicked up my feet. I breathed deep as their voices blurred together in the background.

"Stay behind," I whispered to myself. *Not going to happen.*

Shutting my eyes, I drowned out their conversation. How would Arah and Korland use Osouf's blood to take away Ezrai's power?

In my mind, a crimson-red liquid dripped onto the Ruach. Something powerful in the stone reacted to the king's power. Debris swirled around Korland like a tornado, and the stone sucked the magic out of Ezrai. Would just a drop of Osouf's blood be enough, or would Korland need more?

Suddenly, I saw Osouf again, eyes sunken. Were they slowly

draining him of his blood? A gasp escaped me as my eyelids flew open. *They're going to kill him slowly. That must be how…*

I stood abruptly, then stormed out the door. The crisp, cool air filled my lungs. The rain had let up, leaving behind a light mist that softened the summer heat. We were only a few days away from fall—the night's weather was a taste of what was to come.

Footsteps came after me. Listening closely, I turned my head, just enough to catch a glimpse of his dark hair. Though his breaths weren't quite as deep as usual, there was no doubt who had followed me outside.

"Somehow, I knew it was you," I moaned. My heart sank as I faced Kiran. Questions, lots of them, resurfaced as I stared into those cold green stones that were his eyes. *Why did I rescue him and not my own brother? Could I not have set Osouf free too?*

With a blank expression, Kiran just stood there, arms dangling at his sides. The calm I had once felt around him had dissipated. If anything, his presence made my pulse rise.

"Seems odd, doesn't it?" he asked, a bit of life coming back into his eyes. "Or maybe it's a great ploy. Why would they want to keep Ezrai from tearing down that prison and rescuing your brother?" His lips twisted together in a frown. "Then they say you should stay behind too. What is really going on here?"

What in Elohi was he suggesting?

"Honestly? Who cares?" I shrugged. "It makes sense, I guess. If Raven's information is correct, Ezrai going anywhere near the prison is too risky." Whirling around, I marched forward, grumbling. "What I don't understand is leaving me behind to rescue my own brother. My own brother!"

"Strange," he said. "What is your gut telling you?"

I blinked. "Well, perhaps they think I'm too close to the situation, too emotional." An image of the dead young boy pierced my mind. "I have been…impulsive," I replied in a softer tone. "But there's something else at play."

"And?"

I scratched the back of my neck. "I can't explain it, and it's only speculation—"

"Go on."

"One way or another, Arah and Korland are going to kill Osouf. Either they are slowly draining his blood, or they're waiting to kill him when the time is right. I'm just not sure why."

"Interesting," Kiran said, though it sounded more like a question. "I did hear some talk while I was in the prison about waiting until a blood moon is in the sky."

Blood rushed through my veins. "That's in three days."

"So then, don't waste time," Kiran said.

"What are you suggesting?"

"Do it yourself. Rescue your brother without a word to anyone."

Someone clapped slowly from behind us—I turned to see Robin. She inched closer, a mischievous grin plastered on her face. "Brilliant. I want in."

I sighed, a little relieved. One thing Robin couldn't resist was a challenge.

"I was hoping you'd say that," I said with a smug look.

Robin rested a hand on her hip. "Just don't want you to mess things up *again*." She scrutinized her nails. "I'm just going to make sure you don't screw up. No way I'd leave this task to you on your own."

I bit my tongue in an attempt to ignore her snarky words. "We just need a way to get him out of those chains around his wrists."

"Are they held by a lock?" Robin asked.

"Yes. Any ideas?"

"Why of course, you'll learn just how useful I am soon enough," she grinned. "I have a metal lock-pick I had the old welder make before he passed a few years ago. I keep that and a small knife attached to my crossbow."

"Perfect!" I nearly shouted.

"Alright, then," Kiran said. "I'll make sure the rest of the Sairens are distracted when you two head out. Say, tomorrow evening?"

Robin and I shared a look. Robin raised a brow. "Isn't that the time avros are most active? What kind of plan is that?"

"Exactly why they won't expect you. Besides, how are you supposed to leave the pack in broad daylight without them noticing? They're already on high alert knowing that Lorraine is aching to bust down those walls. She'd do anything to save her brother."

"Fine," I said. "Tomorrow night."

21

ROZLAN, THE LEADER OF THE PACK WHO HAD ASSISTED US WITH the attack on our region, came to Alden to let him know he'd be departing soon. His own territory, Idra Region, had been left to his brother Zeron and wife Elise. Through Rozlan, we learned that Idra too had barely had any incidents in the last few days.

"This silence, it's dangerous," Rozlan told Alden, and the older Sairen wolf concurred. They agreed to be on their guard, and if one of them needed a hand, the signaling howl would send the other to their aid.

Dasan told Robin and me to take a break from training. Likely because Robin had learned to use her power while I still didn't know who I was. Maybe I wasn't capable of knowing.

On the other hand, Dasan had a new lead on finding his daughter, whom I learned had been separated from him the same night that Korland arrived unannounced in Terah Region, kidnapping Osouf and murdering my parents. Dasan said he hadn't seen Evan in several days, since Dasan and Alden had sent him to Korland's prison as a spy to find out more information on Ella. But Evan had yet to report back, so there was no way for Dasan to update Evan that Ella had been transferred. Surely Evan had known by now.

Cylus claimed to have met Ella before but didn't go into detail. The only information he shared was that the young girl was a Shilo, like Kiran, though her abilities were more unique.

Nothing else was said on the matter because Cylus told us it wasn't our main concern. Instead, he and Alden summoned us to form an official plan to save Osouf.

The pack all exchanged their ideas, including Kiran. He played his part well, making suggestions and getting into debates, all the while knowing the three of us had our own plan.

Eventually, someone suggested sneaking Robin in to slowly eradicate Shadow Sairens by Sparking. Cylus and Kiran would escort her. Kiran became so involved in the plan that it was as if he'd forgotten about ours.

"I'm aware we discussed how risky it is to involve the king, but I don't believe we can do this without Ezrai," Kiran said.

"Arah has possession of the stone," Shariee responded. "They'll steal the king's power."

"Which is why I'm proposing we steal the Ruach first. Then the big, bad, mighty wolf can swoop in and make the rest of this rescue mission a piece of cake."

"I would imagine that thing is always with Korland. How do you suggest we steal it?" Cylus, his distaste for Kiran's idea obvious, folded his arms and leaned back in his chair.

"Simple. We follow the plan as discussed. Robin will sneak in, you and myself guiding and protecting her. We'll corner Korland and attack before Robin Sparks." Kiran held his head high. "Then we snatch the stone."

Cylus glared at Kiran, barely blinking. I half expected him to shout back at Kiran. Instead, those silver eyes of his appeared sinister.

"I'll speak with Ezrai," Alden said. "Perhaps he can be on standby. If we succeed in getting the Ruach to him, he'll be close enough to intervene as needed."

The different plans crowded my mind. If they didn't catch Korland off guard, he'd use the staff to hold them down. Then what? If the avros spotted Ezrai, they'd come for him. If Korland already had Osouf's blood, couldn't they steal Ezrai's powers? Alden was correct in it being too risky to involve the king. It was a good thing I had a plan of my own.

Luke entered the den, hair matted. When he saw us all staring at him, the runt ran his fingers through his hair to comb out a few tangles and then plopped down beside his sister.

Shariee grunted.

"What'd I miss?" He smiled as he looked around the room. No one answered him. "Alright, Don't everyone speak at once."

"Maybe if you didn't sleep till noon, you would know," Cylus joked.

"What's with you? If it weren't for the smell of Alden's coffee at 6:23 in the morning, you'd still be sleeping too. You and your sensitive nose." Luke chuckled. Cylus gave him a smile and the other Sairens shared in their laughter.

I wanted to join them, but I remained mute. My chest began to burn, and I jumped to my feet.

"Hello?" I screamed. "Does nobody care about my brother?" I paused. Their expressions were blank, except for Shariee, who looked concerned. I continued, "We finally find out where Osouf is and we change our plans to rescue him, not once, not twice, but over and over again. Here we are yet again, another plan—maybe, possibly—set in motion, and who knows how many more days will pass before we figure this out. I'm sick of it. How can you all just sit here and laugh while you contemplate rescuing Osouf?

Why not just do it?" Letting out an exasperated breath, I dropped my arms to my sides.

No matter, I'll be going myself soon.

To my surprise, Cylus got up calmly and searched my eyes. "Lorraine. I understand."

His words brought flames to my vision. What could he possibly understand?

He inched closer to me. "Nothing will stop you from saving the only family you have left. I know that," he said, hand over his heart. "I lost my family too. If I could go back in time…" His voice wavered, then he growled. "I would have been more careful. No doubt if I had, she would still be here." His jaw trembled as he glanced at Kiran. He froze, then faced me, as if waiting for a response. But I had no words.

"Lorraine," said Alden, "I need Ezrai's approval to include him in this mission. Osouf is important to us too, but this situation is extremely sensitive. We must tread carefully. You understand, don't you?"

I couldn't move or speak. Sound began to fade, until all I could hear was a heartbeat. Something pulsed through me.

"Lorraine," the voice called.

My legs wobbled. There was an orange flash before the lights went out.

A tiny glow filtered through my lashes as my eyes opened cautiously. Shariee sat on the couch, playing with a ribbon in her hand. No one else was present, so I sat up. Her head turned slightly while her eyes remained focused on the ribbon.

"You're awake," she said cheerfully.

"Yeah. Where is everyone?"

"Well, almost everyone went to speak with the king. Robin is visiting her family and Luke is somewhere outside. Playing around, probably." She giggled, then put down the ribbon—now tied in a knot—and came over to feel my forehead. "So…you feeling okay? What happened?"

The meaning of her earlier sentence suddenly dawned. "They know where Ezrai is? Wait, I want to go!" I shot up and stumbled towards the door. "Where do I go?"

"Slow down, Lorraine." Shariee put her arm out to stop me. "He appeared to Dasan recently, and finally let him know where he's residing."

"And where is that? They didn't know before when he showed up in Hyra village after the attack?" I asked.

"In the Caves of Luta. From what I understand, they're northeast of Hyra. And no, we didn't get to visit with the king for long at that time. He said he'd return soon, and sure enough he did."

"Funny how I keep missing opportunities to meet this king of ours," I said, a bit calmer.

"Mmhm. So, what happened earlier? How come you passed out?"

"Not sure. If I explain it to you, I'll seem crazy." My head ached.

"Try me," she said.

"I keep seeing flames." I took a deep breath. Enthusiasm sparked in her eyes. "It's like a mighty fire that builds up in my veins until it's so strong, so intoxicating that I end up becoming…weak."

"Well, that's interesting. I'm not sure what that could mean. It sounds worrisome though." Shariee bit her nails, a habit of hers.

Shariee's gaze turned distant. She must think I'd lost my mind, but at least I'd finally confessed. Now that I had told someone my secret, everything was spilling out.

"Right. That's not all, though." I captured her attention again. "There's this voice. It's calling me. I can't explain how, but I know it wants me to go after Osouf. I have to go. Sitting around and waiting for the pack to bring home Osouf is not an option for me."

"Lorraine," Shariee said softly. "Don't take this the wrong way, but you can be a bit impulsive sometimes. Maybe try…not to, this time?" Her bright-amber eyes made me glance up.

"Look, I've made some faulty decisions lately. Obviously, they've cost us. But this feels different. Shariee, you have to believe me. Something tells me I need to go after Osouf myself."

"Okay, fine." She sighed. "Whatever you need. What can I do to help?"

"Just give me a head start. Robin is coming with me. We'll sneak out tonight. Let the pack know in the morning. If we don't return by then, send backup."

Hesitantly, she agreed, "Alright."

It wasn't long before the sun began to set. Robin was conveniently back from seeing her family, and the rest of the pack had yet to return from their trip to speak with Ezrai.

Shariee distracted Luke in another room. Robin's and my mission to sneak off was a simple task. A little too easy, but we seized the opportunity anyway and headed for the prison.

22

THE EVENING AIR WAS A BIT COOLER. THE BREEZE CHILLED MY skin, giving me a break from the late summer heat. Fall was already starting, which had the two of us carefully stepping around fallen leaves. The trees had begun shifting colors, from green to brown, red, and orange.

Robin's crossbow was strapped to her back along with her leather quiver. Before leaving the cabin, she stressed that her Sparking powers were a last resort, especially now that we knew the avros could be turned back to human. Robin would learn that ability in time, as Ezrai had promised.

She had no problem with using her Sparking powers on the Shadow Sairens, though. Thankfully, she had gathered more tranquilizing serum for her crossbolt bolts from Raven earlier. She explained the serum was made from a mixture of moonflower and mushrooms. Something about the way the moonflower reacts to mushrooms when heated together in water creates a liquid that could make one fatigued and fall asleep within seconds. The new Sairen wolf struggled with the idea of killing, even monsters.

The trail grew darker as we traveled through the woods; thankfully, my nose never failed me.

The woods were ominously silent, which caused both Robin and me to flinch at every crunch of a leaf or rustling of wildlife here and there. I couldn't shake the feeling of being followed.

"How long have we got?" she asked.

"About another hour, I'd say."

"Not too bad."

We walked up a steep hill. If it weren't for the crossbow on Robin's back, we could easily fly over it. But Robin made long strides up the hill without grumbling.

"So," she started. "You brought back Kiran and not your own brother? Must be in love."

"It's not like that," I snapped.

"Well, if you say so."

Over the hill now, I picked up my pace, leaving her to follow behind instead of beside me.

"Acting that way only proves it."

I spun on my heels to look her straight in the eyes. "You know, there was something about him that I did admire, something that made me feel…calm, for once." The words spewed from my mouth. "Well, things are different now. I can barely look at him. I'm constantly reminded that I had a chance to get Osouf out of there, and I failed to do it."

Besides, Kiran had been different lately. I turned back around and continued down the path. A familiar scent filled my nose. Robin matched my speed, then suddenly threw her arm out in front of my stomach. Her wide eyes scanned our surroundings. "Did you hear that?" she whispered.

My ears tuned in to the sounds of the forest. A small buzz from some sort of insect was all I could make out.

Without warning, Raven stepped out from behind a tree with a sharp grin and wild eyes. "Robin."

My head turned swiftly to each side as I searched for the avro in control of her mind. I couldn't detect any.

"It has to be here somewhere," I said.

Robin appeared speechless, her eyes fixed on Raven. Could Robin sense that her cousin was not quite herself? She remained still, as if waiting to hear what Raven had to say.

Raven took a few steps closer to us. "Robin, we need you back home." Her voice was tinged with desperation, yet her expression was neutral.

She began to casually walk towards us. My hand flinched, transforming me to four legs. I flapped my wings in irritation as Robin's hand flew in front of my face, stopping me in my tracks once again. "Wait," she hissed.

Raven sighed as she stopped to glare at us. The muscle at the corner of her mouth twitched, though her eyes glistened.

"Come on, would you really come at your own?" Raven taunted as she tilted her head.

Slowly, Robin spun her crossbow around to her chest. Knowing the weapon had a tranquilizing dart loaded, I returned to human form. Putting her cousin to sleep would give us time to find the monster responsible for corrupting Raven's mind again.

Surely the avro controlling Raven was close by and would either attack or make a run for it. I glanced over my shoulder and around, ready for a chase. But as I sniffed the air, I could scent no avro.

From the corner of my eye, I saw Robin take out the crossbow dart and replace it with a regular bolt.

She'll kill her.

My head whipped around. "Robin!" I yelled, though she was standing right next to me. "Don't—"

But it was too late. Her finger had curled around the trigger, releasing the bolt.

I blinked. Raven was hit above her left breast. She grinned, gripping the bolt. In an instant, she dissolved into black smoke.

Robin's hand trembled as she lowered her weapon. Both of us stood there in shock.

"How?" I questioned Robin, tripping over my own words. "How did you know?"

"Raven has a pale birthmark on her right shoulder. Pretty easy to see in contrast to her dark skin. But this thing…" Robin frowned and her lip curled. "This thing had the birthmark on her left shoulder." She secured the crossbow to her back. "I knew it couldn't be her."

Anxiety grew inside of me; its fists banged against my chest. The eerie scene fogged my mind. What had we just witnessed? If there were more of these creatures, who else would they portray?

Black smoke collected in front of us, thickening, with red, glowing eyes at its center.

"Alright, Robin. Now would be a good time to Spark," I suggested.

She nodded, tossed her crossbow and quiver away, and then took her stance in wolf form. White electricity branched out into the fog. Like lightning, it brightened the forest, giving us a fleeting view of the many Shadow Sairens stalking us. About a hundred more red eyes filled the darkened space.

Robin sent another shock wave through them, dissolving a dozen. Gritting her teeth, she gathered more strength and Sparked a third time, and then a fourth. Each breath seemed to grow more ragged than the last.

Returning to human form, I picked up her bow. I called to her in a hushed tone, hoping it wouldn't draw the Shadows closer. "We should make a run for it."

In response, Robin molded herself into human form. Keeping her eyes on the Shadow Sairens, Robin took a few steps back, holding her hand out for her precious crossbow and bolts. I placed it in her hand, keeping an eye on the Shadow Sairens while she strapped her items in place over her shoulder. Robin leaned back, eyes never straying from the glowing red orbs.

"On the count of three," she said.

I nodded, though she couldn't see me.

"One…"

In unison, both of us took a small step back.

"Two…"

A few more steps.

"Three!"

Swiftly, I spun and darted forward. I kept moving as fast as I could, maneuvering around the trees. It would be easier with four legs, but Robin said she wanted to hold onto her crossbow bolts. I felt tempted to flick my wrist. Except that would leave my packmate behind.

The black, wolf-shaped smoke appeared in my peripheral vision. Sharp pains invaded my chest as I tried to control my breathing: in through the nose, out the mouth. More pain spread through my ribs.

They stayed right on our tail. The fog glided closer, but never fully surrounded us. *Are they running us to exhaustion so they can attack us when we're weak?*

A Shadow Sairen suddenly formed in front of me.

I covered my mouth and ran straight through it. The wolf broke up into a cloud. I dared not breathe it in. When the coast was clear, I removed my hand, the night air filling my lungs.

"Lorraine!" Robin screamed from nearby. "You gotta Spark! There's too many."

She was Sparking again herself. Flashes of her power reached throughout the poisonous fog. It was enough to make them retreat a little, if only temporarily.

A sinister growl vibrated among the evil creatures.

We were so close to Osouf, so close to the place where the Ruach was being held. What frightened me the most was losing the only family I had left. Though, losing ourselves and the entire world to these monsters would, without a doubt, be worse. Too much was at stake with this mission.

"Robin!" I shouted back. "Gather up as much power as you can. On the count of three, we'll run through them."

"Are you crazy?" she snapped.

"A little, but what choice do we have? Our powers will reach more Shadow Sairens the closer we get to them. Just be sure to hold your breath."

"And what if you can't Spark?"

"I will. Now get ready," I urged.

I didn't know if my powers would come to me. But I was hopeful. My heart pounded, adrenaline surging through me.

Neriah, Ezrai, please help us.

23

WE DOVE STRAIGHT INTO THE PORTENTOUS DARKNESS THAT flooded the forest. The initial entrance into the fog sent tiny, invisible spikes down my nostrils and into my lungs. It didn't stop me. I could once again feel the warmth of the power deep within. We pushed further into the mass of black shadows.

As if we'd broken some sort of barrier, a loud crack filled the air. Gold light radiated around us, scattering the poisonous wolves.

Was that me?

Robin and I coughed as we pulled ourselves upright and transformed into humans. A red-and-orange hue flickered on the ground, so I crouched down to investigate. A small flame burned by my feet.

There was something odd about the flame, though. It sat on top of a fallen leaf, but didn't seem to be burning it, or anything around it. I picked up the leaf with steady hands, careful to not put out the flame.

"Woooo."

Robin's holler startled me, making me let go of the leaf and juggling to keep the flame from falling. It was pointless; the strange fire disappeared once it hit the ground. I stood.

"I cannot believe that actually worked," she said as she approached me, putting out her hand for me to shake. "I can't believe you Sparked." Her hand gripped mine tight as she searched my eyes. "That was you, right?"

The scene replayed in my mind. At least, the parts that my brain could make sense of. Electricity and heat pumped through my veins. Still, the moment just before the thunder—all that energy was gone. It didn't exactly feel released, more like dissipated.

"I don't...know," was all I managed to say.

Robin seemed to accept my response, trudging on toward the Alcazar. I followed her. Both of us were winded, our feet moving slower with every step.

"Shall we stop and take a break?" Robin suggested.

"Of course not."

"You are a stubborn one, aren't you?" she retorted.

"Call it what you want, I just don't tire easily," I scoffed.

"Whatever you say, dog."

A coy smile stretched my lips. "You're one of us now." I couldn't help but laugh a little.

"Fair," Robin said, her shoulders relaxing. "But, you tend to do things before thinking. We should take a small breather before busting down those walls."

Regaining our strength for what was ahead *was* the smart thing to do. The future of Elohi was at stake. Dasan's words echoed in my head. *Be slow to anger.*

I relented. We leaned our backs against a nearby tree for a few minutes. It wasn't until we got up, stretched, and began walking again that Robin spoke.

"Can I ask you something?"

"Knowing you, you'd ask either way."

"You mentioned Kiran was different lately," she began.

"Did I say that?" I interrupted.

"Not exactly, but one could gather by your words that something changed…did it not?"

"Yeah, I guess." My eyes widened as I understood her meaning. Except, it wasn't possible. "If you're referring to what happened back there with Raven's evil twin, I doubt Kiran has one."

As we reached the large clearing in the forest that housed our destination, I pulled Robin behind a tree so the avros didn't spot us.

"During the fight in Hyra, I followed them here," I explained. "It wasn't long before I snuck in and got Kiran out of there. Could that have been enough time to duplicate him?"

Robin slid her crossbow to her chest and aimed at the avros guarding the prison.

"I understand what you mean, though," I said. "It raises the question of who else has been copied and made into some freakish reflection of themselves."

As I finished my sentence, Robin hit her first target. "My question is," Robin started as she aimed at her next target. "How?" Another avro fell to its knees. "We really don't know what is *possible* at this point, do we?"

Our path was clear. Instead of answering, I waved for her to follow me onward. Once I got to the spot I'd seen Korland stand and give the secret passage, I leaned forward, speaking clearly but not too loudly. "Est therin."

Since Robin and I approached from the top of a slight hill, the entry from the rooftop became somewhat visible. I ran through our plan one last time.

"Once we reach Osouf, you go find Korland. Use your bolt to knock him out and snatch the staff. Then meet me on the roof."

"Sounds simple...and like everything is about to go wrong," said Robin.

"Let it be known now, you were aware of everything going wrong." I let out a small snicker.

"You got that lock pick I gave you?" Robin asked. I nodded and then looked ahead.

A cool breeze blew, but did not remove the sweat from my neck. The one thing I hated about the human form.

More Shadow Sairens surrounded the Alcazar, but it was no problem. Robin summoned her Sparking powers and ran up to the black wolves, letting out several flashes of light.

"Hmph," said Robin when she returned. "And Kiran thought we needed Ezrai for this?"

"You have no idea what lingers inside; I'm not so sure I myself know everything that's there. For our sakes, it would be nice if he was here right now. Not to mention, I'd like to see this king for myself." I mumbled the last bit.

Because we needed her crossbow and bolts for Korland, once I was in Sairen wolf form, Robin hitched a ride to the top of the building.

Once inside, we scoured each room. The first two were empty. The only items we found were papers with gibberish written on them and a tall, dusty mirror leaning against the wall.

"You recognize this language?" Robin asked. She raised her brow as she handed me a document.

I shook my head. "Do the avros have their own language or something?"

I took a closer look at it. The words were foreign to me. Possibly they were the ancient Sairen language.

Chains rattled from the other side of the door. I was suddenly reminded of why we were here. A sense of urgency came rushing back. I crumpled the paper and grabbed the door handle.

"There are prisoners on the other side; hopefully, most are

asleep. So be quiet."

"Got it."

Pushing the door slowly only sent an obnoxious creaking sound bouncing around the cells. I held my breath, hoping it wouldn't wake any of the prisoners. Something stirred in one of the cells, but it was too dark to tell which one. Both of us stilled, and I worked on controlling my breathing.

We moved on. In one cell, one avro was wide awake, staring at us. The door to the cell was open, indicating that she was not there against her free will, but keeping guard.

I put my finger in front of my lips, threatening her not to make a sound as I pointed at Robin's weapon with my other hand. The guard backed up as we entered her cell, Robin's crossbow pointed at her heart.

"Korland's staff," I whispered in a harsh tone. "Where is it?"

The creature held her hands up in surrender, but she smiled. "It's okay. Kill me." She looked to the crossbow with an almost hopeful expression.

Robin gave me a side glance, waiting for my approval.

"Can't do that just yet," I said. "We need to know where the staff is. So spill." I marched closer to the avro, prepared to make her talk. The sun started to peer through the only tiny window in the cell room. We were running out of time.

She gave a small giggle, then cocked her head to the side and said, "Oh, dear. Even if I tell you where it is, you won't find it. Korland is waiting for you; you're falling right into his trap. No turning back now."

I searched her eyes for any humanity left. How long had she been an avro? Was there any fight left in her at all?

Robin didn't take any chances. She used one of her sleeping darts to knock out the guard. Frustrated, I dropped my arms and groaned softly.

"What?" she said, sarcasm in her voice. "We're wasting time."

Apparently realizing she was no longer whispering, Robin pursed her lips, but it was too late. The other prisoners were awake.

We ran from the open cell and through to the other side of the door. Fear, excitement, and curiosity assaulted me all at once as I faced the only thing standing between Osouf and myself. Noticing my apprehension, Robin moved closer.

"This is it," I said. "Osouf is on the other side. Are you sure you're okay going alone from this point?"

Robin looked around the hallway, making sure no one was lurking. She faced me, tapping her weapon and grinning. "Got these babies. Besides, we agreed I would be the distraction."

"How many do you have left?"

"Four. Two regulars and two specials," she said confidently. "I'll be sure to keep one special for Korland. Now go on. Hurry up and go to the rooftop when you've got Osouf. I'll meet you there."

"This is stupid. You know that, right?"

"I don't think it is." Robin scanned the hallway again. "The way I see it, if I'm the distraction, and you two get away, then Korland won't have who may potentially be the red wolf. If you're the distraction, I may have a chance at stealing the Ruach."

"If you can even find it," I said. "Just, please be careful."

Robin scrunched her lips. "There are a lot of unknowns, so just shut up and go free your brother already."

I nodded and made my way into the room where Osouf was being held after picking the lock. It was pitch dark. My hand glided over the walls for guidance. I could hear someone's shallow breathing. My hand continued to move along the wall, and I prayed for light. Something, someone, was in here. Osouf?

Finally, I came across a lantern with a low glow. I worked with it in repetition to fan the flame and silently cheered when the flame grew brighter.

With the lantern in hand, I turned around to shed some light over whoever—

I breathed hard, my cheeks hot. There he was, standing there waiting. Dark hair, green eyes, and calloused flesh. His overgrown bat wings arched over his head.

Korland was waiting for me.

24

THE URGE TO LEAP AT KORLAND AND TEAR HIM TO SHREDS GREW inside me. Except, the red stone on his staff caught my attention. Impulsive actions wouldn't get me anywhere, so I ground my teeth instead, glaring at him. The memory of my parents' deaths flashed in my mind. My throat felt thick.

Usually, my recollection of my parents' killer was blurry, but now the monster stood in front of me, plain as day. The grey in his hair, the texture on his wings, and those all-too-familiar green eyes. Without tears flooding my vision, or anger blinding me, I could see him clearly. He wasn't fully avro, but still human. Did he fight the darkness deep within? His movements were almost human-like.

But the most obvious sign of his humanity was his eyes. Korland's eyes were not purple, like a number of avros I'd seen. He had embraced the darkness, but somewhere inside flickered a tiny spark of the person he used to be.

My skin crawled. Suddenly, I no longer cared about the staff.
"Where is my brother?" I demanded.

"Getting ready," he said sharply. "You see, thanks to you, Lord Arah is about to rule this world."

Furious, I locked eyes with him, though it sent a shiver down my spine. "What are you talking about? I'll kill you!"

A cackling rumbled in his belly. "Oh, you are too much fun," he mocked. "Arah wanted your brother dead, because of some stupid dream some lunatic Sairen wolf had that one born under a blood moon would destroy him. They named this special being the 'red wolf.'" Korland's eyes rolled. "But then Arah heard of Ezrai's appearance and realized, he is the one we're after. With this precious bit of blood…" He rolled a glass tube stoppered with a cork between his fingers.

I gasped.

Korland took painfully slow, menacing steps toward me. "My sources told me you don't have any powers. You have nothing I need." He faced me, and I spat at him.

He jerked back, wiping his face. He let out an abrupt roar.

"Where is my brother?" I screamed, ready to burst into tears at any second.

Looking exasperated, the monster picked up his staff and used its power to pin me down, holding me in place.

"Ezrai is coming," he sneered. "Maybe not today, or tomorrow, but he followed you here and I know he's waiting for his opportunity."

"You're wrong; he didn't follow me. He's not coming." Even as I said it, I hoped Ezrai might come with the pack to rescue me.

Korland lunged forward and pulled my hair back, bending my neck. "Oh, but see, you're wrong. I sent my shadow dogs after you; only one returned to tell the tale. Your precious king came to save you."

Ezrai. The golden electricity belonged to him. How did

Robin not recognize it? She'd seen his power before.

Korland released me. "Your brother is no longer here."

My stomach churned. Was he alive, or had he escaped? Osouf was clever. But after all this time, how would he finally make it out?

"What do you mean?" I questioned, my jaw tight.

The staff relented, freeing me. Korland's face went blank for a moment and then he hit the side of his head. "Stop!" he cried. Korland's green eyes searched my face. "I didn't kill him. I–I let him go, just as you got here." He stumbled back. "Why did I do that?" he shouted, this time pressing both hands against his ears and letting out a scream. *Osouf is free?*

Once again, the darkness in Korland shifted. He dragged himself upright. "Now, where was I?"

A knock on the door interrupted our conversation. Once the creature walked into the room, I could see that it was Evan. He cowered in Korland's presence, his hands holding chains, which dragged behind him.

"He-here you g-go, sir." Evan stumbled, averting his eyes from mine.

Confused, I watched him hand over the linked metal. If Evan was really on our side, he wouldn't be helping Korland. But then again, this could be part of Evan's mission, to be a spy. Had he learned anything about Ella?

Just as Korland gripped his staff once more, I swiftly took Sairen wolf form and lunged at Korland. My teeth landed in his arm. Angry, Korland shook me off and pushed me back with the aid of his magical staff. While holding me down, he commanded Evan to quickly lock me in the chains. Suddenly, I was human again as Evan placed the metal cuffs around my wrists.

The metal clanked as I shook the chains. I tried fighting against the force of his staff, pulling at the chains, though they cut into my skin. A furious growl escaped me as I struggled to break free.

"I'll have to say thank you to my son for bringing you to me." Korland grinned, watching me, as if waiting for my reaction.

I gave him a blank stare. The identity of his son was a mystery to me.

He carefully slid his claw around the line of my jaw. "Aw, you don't know, do you?"

A vicious growl vibrated my chest, releasing through my clamped teeth. My face muscles twitched as the point of his claw ripped my skin. But I couldn't move away.

Korland tilted his head in a way that made my insides boil.

I gasped. "It can't be."

"Oh? It can. And it is," he hissed. "Kiran—well, the real Kiran—is indeed my son."

My most recent meal surged up my throat. I swallowed it back down. Despite everything we'd discovered in the past week, I still couldn't believe it. Kiran was a Sairen wolf.

Though the more Korland's words echoed in my brain, the more the pieces fell into place. Since Kiran was rescued, we'd never seen him in his wolf form.

Robin was right. I wasn't sure how, but in a matter of minutes they'd made a reflection of him and allowed that creature to be rescued. So Kiran would convince us to bring Ezrai here? To fall into Korland's trap?

The monster wrapped his fingers around my neck. "Now, if you'll excuse me, your friend is wreaking havoc in my castle. Oh Kiran?" he sang, summoning the imposter from the other side of the door. It opened the door immediately, waiting for Korland's next command.

Korland left the room, along with Evan. Meanwhile, I was chained in place, with this so-called "Kiran" being. Though I had my suspicions, once I fixed my eyes on the direction his hair swayed, it became evident to me. This *thing*, it really was a reflection of Kiran.

"What are you?" I asked the creature.

He crossed his arms and leaned against the wall. "The name's Kiran."

"No. You're a reflection of him." I clamped my teeth together. "Where is the real Kiran?"

"Locked up, of course."

"How are you living? What are you?" I demanded.

"Ah," he said, looking away from me. "Darkness. Negative energy can create things. Arah made us with his darkness."

"I don't understand." Blood pounded inside my head, heightening my frustration.

His eyes found mine again. "I'm a Shadow Sairen. Specifically, Kiran's shadow, or reflection, as you call it."

I stopped drilling the creature for information. The discomfort of the metal holding me down grew by the minute. Finally, Korland and Evan came back with an unconscious Robin. An intense glare was all I could give to a traitor assisting the enemy.

After my packmate was chained the same as me, Korland leaned in, his hot breath tickling my ear. "And now we wait for Ezrai."

I tried to bite him, but he moved back just in time. "Why not just kill us?" I asked.

Evan stood behind Korland with one hand over his mouth and the other waving at me, as if urging me to not say anything else. Korland slashed my face with his claws. My cheeks stung as my skin ripped open and blood dripped down my face. A few drops landed on my feet and leg, the rest sticking to my hair.

"I've already explained this," he hissed. "How can you be saved if you're dead?"

For quite some time, he just stared at me. I studied him carefully. *Why would Ezrai come save me now when Osouf has been here all this time?*

My mouth fell open. I wiggled in my chains. "You can't do

it, can you? Kill me? But why...you—you killed my parents. Why not me?"

The monster shook his head, wiping his chin. "My son has taken a liking to you and your friends." Korland's words sounded like they'd been torn from his throat.

He tensed, grabbing his head. Something rumbled in his throat and he heaved a little as he seemed to regain his composure.

A whispering sound came from the stone in his staff. Korland gripped the staff and turned his back on us, making his way out of the room along with the reflection of Kiran and Evan. A red glow flickered from the Ruach, along with more whispers.

"Ezrai is watching," it said.

25

My hands grew numb. Next to me, Robin stirred. She moaned inaudible words, her wrists rotating as she presumably felt the cold, restricting metal.

"This is all your fault," Robin mumbled grumpily.

"I thought we already discussed how risky this plan was," I scoffed.

She snorted as she continued to wiggle around. The more she tried to break free, the angrier she grew. The chains wouldn't budge. Robin let out a high-pitched groan. "When I get out of these chains…"

"What? What are you gonna do?"

"Whatever I can do." She seemed to calm. "At least one good thing has come out of this. I was able to find the real Kiran and set him free. Told him to run and go get help. But then Korland spotted me."

"Well, at least there's that." I stared at the ground. I tried to lift my head, but my thoughts weighed it down. *Kiran is Korland's son.*

Robin pulled at her chains…again. "What now, oh brilliant one?"

I searched the room in hopes that something of use would stand out to me. Nothing. "Can you Spark?" I asked.

She squirmed, tiny lightning bolts forming down her arms. Then she yanked the chains repeatedly. "It's no use. Sparking in human form doesn't have the same power."

The room grew quiet. There wasn't any sound from the other side of the door, either. The stillness felt eerie, like the calm before the storm. I could sense Robin's uneasiness as well.

"You know why my family have bird names?" she suddenly asked.

I thought for a moment—I hadn't noticed that. "Why?"

"It was Grandma's idea," Robin began. "Her name was Maggie, but Grandpa called her his magpie."

"Ah. Like the bird."

"Exactly." She stared off to the side, as though lost in a memory. "He died. Grandpa…became an avro. No one saw it coming. He was the most gentle and light-hearted human being. It just didn't seem possible. It caught us all off guard."

"You knew him? Or did he die before you were born?"

"I was seven when he died. The name thing started because Grandma would always say she dreamed of flying. She loved birds. They would sit outside early in the morning just to watch them and listen. That's why Grandpa gave her the magpie nickname. From there, they decided to name their two sons, as you know, Falcon and Finch. My dad and uncle continued the tradition." Robin pulled at her chains again.

"So, what happens when you run out of bird names?" I teased, trying to keep her distracted.

At first, it seemed as though I'd lost her, as she was fixated on her chains. But, after huffing, she relaxed and hung her head.

"No idea," Robin said, a bit out of breath. "You know, it was a Sairen wolf that killed him." Her words surprised me until she clarified. "Grandpa."

"Oh," I whispered. Suddenly, Robin's distrust of us made sense. Her anger and determination made her a fierce warrior. One who would save even the humans who lost their way and turned. She was a real hero. I couldn't consider myself the same.

"Well, I do admit, thanks to you we saved a few humans who'd turned."

"*We*?" Her voice went up an octave. "You were reluctant to help. Thought I was crazy."

Wiggling my wrist in the chains, I was suddenly reminded of when I first met Robin.

"The wrist thing..." I started. "How did you know our transformation is activated by the right wrist?"

"Oh, that," Robin muttered. "I just happened to notice every Sairen used their right wrist when transforming, that's all."

"Do you know about the glow?" I asked. Robin formed a puzzled expression.

"Glow? What—"

Before either of us could say another word, Evan barged in and barred the door behind him. The avro sank to the floor, catching his breath. Banging followed, with voices behind the door demanding the traitor open it.

"Care to fill us in?" Robin asked.

Evan, still trembling, pulled himself up. "I..." His eyes widened. "They were onto me." One arm grabbed the other, as if he were holding himself together. "Korland had his guards watch my every move. W-what was I supposed to do?"

The noise behind the door grew louder, the unified strength of whoever was on the other side loosening the hinges. Evan moved quickly. Robin's quiver was slung over his shoulder. In one hand he had her crossbow. He opened his other fist, and on his palm was a key. The avro shakily placed the key in each cuff, releasing both Robin and myself. He returned Robin's weapons to her.

"You should probably go now. But before you do, I think there's something you should know…about Arah's plans for Ella."

One of the hinges busted off the door. Any second, they would break through. Robin and I exchanged a look.

"Wait," I said. "Aren't you coming with us?"

"I have to distract them, or they'll come after—"

The door flew open. As a handful of avros leaped over the broken pieces, time seemed to move slowly. The avros left the door wide open and we could hear more monsters in the distance. I made eye contact with Evan, who gave me a wry smile. "I'm not scared," he mouthed.

The avros lunged at him while I just stood there, gaping. Robin pulled on my arm.

"Evan!" I cried. "You're still human."

Robin tore off a rusted bar and bent the other that covered the window and broke the glass. We crawled out, leaping down with the help of our wings.

I exhaled. *We made it…but Evan didn't, and there's no way to know what he found out about Ella.*

TWO AVRO GUARDS APPEARED SURPRISED AS WE DROPPED IN FRONT of them. Robin didn't waste time. She grabbed two darts in each hand and walked right up to the avros, sticking the darts between the avros' necks and shoulders.

"You'll thank me later," she whispered to them as they tumbled to the ground.

We ran to the edge of the woods, ducking behind a bush. We sat there a moment, just breathing in the fresh air and processing everything. The more I thought of Evan, the more my anger mounted.

"Couldn't you have Sparked?" I said. "We could have rescued Evan. Why didn't you let me help him?"

"Does this really need to be explained?" Robin rubbed her temples. "Sparking would have sent an army of avros after us had they noticed the bright light from beyond the door. Besides..." She started but paused to look away from me. "By the time we could process what was happening, it was too late. He was already...gone." She straightened. "Evan made his decision. The best we can do is honor it."

"You're cold, you know that?" I scoffed. But she was right. I'd still wanted to try and save him, though it wouldn't have mattered. By the time I realized the avros had busted through the door, Evan was gone...and I knew that when I cried out to him.

Ignoring me, Robin whirled around. A strong breeze blew strands of hair into our faces. When it stopped, the world seemed to stall.

Neither of us moved. I was certain Robin felt it too—Ezrai? Our heads turned simultaneously. The sight of him was something I could never have prepared myself for. Even at a distance, the king seemed to be three times the size of any average Sairen wolf.

I gawked at him. His fur, white as snow, had a brilliant shine that made him seem unreal. His wingspan was enormous, though it would make the king an easy target. Yet, none of those things were as mesmerizing as the radiant red design imprinted on his forehead. Three crescent moons interlocked together, glowing from the inside.

"Is that really..."

"Yes, that's him," Robin replied. "It still amazes me." She paused. "The sight of him."

Ezrai approached Korland's prison, breaking my trance. But this was a trap, and Robin hadn't succeeded in snatching the Ruach.

"We have to stop him!" I shouted. Without waiting for a response from Robin, I leaped down the small hill, running as fast as I could on two legs. It wasn't until I reached Ezrai that the possibility of transforming came to mind, but I was already in front of Ezrai, blocking his way.

Up close, he was even more intimidating. My mouth opened

without speaking. I swallowed and tried again, this time blurting out the words.

"You can't. You can't use your powers here. Korland has your Ruach, and—and—" My words began to jumble together. "I'm safe, Osouf is free somewhere, and Kiran, I think…"

The king's expression was relaxed. He calmly glanced over at Robin, who I could hear approaching from behind. My puzzlement grew.

"Do you think you and your brother are the only ones worth saving?" Ezrai inquired.

"Of course not," I answered. "But Ezrai, we need you. If your powers are taken—"

"Lorraine." He spoke with a firm, yet serene tone. "I know the path I am taking." For a moment, I found myself lost again at the sight of him. My rapidly beating heart slowed. I breathed freely as a weight was lifted from within me.

This is our king, the one to which our race belonged, the one prophesied to lead us to victory.

As the king's head turned to look back at the Sairen wolves now joining him, Osouf appeared by his side in human form, along with Rozlan and his pack.

I fumbled to find the right words. Instead, I stood there, wide-mouthed, stunned. My heart fluttered with excitement. If only these legs of mine would move.

I assessed my brother's condition, disappointment sinking in. Osouf didn't look himself; his face was sallow, his eyes faintly swollen, and grime coated his cheekbones. Even so, my brother stood there smirking, like he was about to tease me.

Placing his fists on his hips, Osouf leaned over, raising an eyebrow. "Miss me?" Those dark eyes of his were livelier than ever.

Typical. Nothing phases him.

I chuckled softly. Nothing had really changed—he was still the same brother I knew. I ran to him and flung my arms around him.

"You wish," I teased, squeezing him a little tighter and letting out a deep sigh of relief.

Moving aside, I watched the guard avros tremble at the sight of the king–allowing Ezrai to continue inside the prison. The shadow Sairens ran at him, but vaporized when they touched him.

My focus shifted back to Osouf. "Where did you—"

"Let's not worry about that right now. There'll be plenty of time to go over it later," he said. "For now, our job is to guard the king's back while he does his thing."

Then I noticed the rest of the pack—all in Sairen wolf form—flanking Ezrai in a curved formation, ready to defend him. My heart skipped a beat as a familiar grey wolf with black ears and a black tail stood beside the king.

Kiran? It had to be the real him, since he was standing there as a Sairen wolf.

Robin leaned in, placing her hand on my shoulder—I jumped. "That's your brother?" she asked, her eyes on Osouf, but I didn't respond. Robin let out a "Hmpf" and then casually found a place to stand with the pack.

It was impressive to see everyone standing there, their eyes fixed ahead. Even Luke held his head high behind the king, though he nervously whistled to himself. In human form, hands behind his back, Dasan stepped beside King Ezrai. Ezrai gave a confirming nod to Dasan.

"Off we go," Dasan said, transforming to Sairen wolf. Ezrai marched forward, leading everyone to the Alcazar.

Once we approached the main door, a thunderous roar came from Ezrai. "Korland." Every word packed a powerful punch. "Open. These. Cages."

I glided over to the doorway, maneuvering to the king's side. Korland came out of the building with a sly grin plastered on his face. He stopped in front of Ezrai and didn't move an inch. He stood there, face to face with the most powerful Sairen wolf of all. Kiran's father gripped his staff with a steady hand.

Eying the red stone, I thought of ways to snatch it. *If I'm quick enough, with Korland focused on Ezrai…could I?*

I had to act fast. Except, in an instant, dozens of avros surrounded us.

"Come on, *oh powerful one*," Korland taunted. "We both know you don't need me to set them all free. Go ahead, save them." Korland playfully twisted the staff in his hand.

Without hesitation, Ezrai spoke. "Open. These. Cages." At each word, golden electricity flowed from his body, sending a wave throughout the prison. Awestruck at the beauty of it, I almost didn't feel the shock that threw me to the floor. However, flames flooded my vision as his power struck me.

Through blurry eyes, I saw how the staff sucked the golden electricity inside the stone.

Everything became muted.

The Ruach glowed brighter now, but the black cloud inside still lingered. *Is it from the staff's power?* Korland regained his balance and shook himself. At least half of the avros were human again, but the rest's eyes were filled with an even greater darkness than before.

Humans scurried to escape the prison. In the midst of all the chaos, Ezrai transformed, his human shape blending in with the crowd. His dark hair and cinnamon-colored skin were a stark contrast to his white Sairen wolf form.

My hearing returned as he walked over to me, extending his hand.

"Come with me," he said, his kind eyes smiling at me.

As I grabbed his hand, pulling myself up, I glanced over at Korland. It was as though some invisible force was keeping him from stepping forward. Though he proudly held the staff, something clearly kept him from using its power.

"Shouldn't we grab your stone?" I suggested.

The king pursed his lips. "Don't fret. He has no control over the Ruach. Besides, Arah is nearby." Ezrai looked me in the eyes. "Not to worry," he reassured me. "In due time."

We returned to the pack, who all seemed startled by the course of events. None of them were looking at us; no, they were gazing above our heads. The sky was painted with shades of orange and red. The most terrifying sight was the sun. Or was it the moon that burned the color of blood?

As we arrived at the cabin, Alden guided us to sit down and then looked Ezrai directly in the eye.

"Alright, what say you? What's the damage?"

The king nodded. "You all will notice, once I'm in my Sairen wolf form again, that only two of my crescent moons glow, and one no longer. This is because different portions of my power are linked to them. Through the staff, Arah has gained one. With two, I still have a great amount of power, and healing capabilities, but if I were to be down to one, I'd grow weaker each day." Ezrai looked around the room. "All I would have left are my healing powers, but my strength will fade."

The world had darkened, and although my hands were red with guilt, Ezrai had chosen to show up. He had made the decision to risk himself. *But why?*

A somber atmosphere hovered inside Alden's home. Everyone was quiet until Luke walked by Cylus and tripped over his own feet.

"Aw come on, you tripped me," Luke whined. Cylus only huffed, shaking his head to indicate he did no such thing.

"Thank you, Ezrai, for filling us in," Alden said, ignoring the runt. "Everyone, please, make yourselves comfortable." The older Sairen went for his usual chair as the rest of us got situated, spaced out in the process. The room grew quiet once again.

I glanced up at Kiran, only to find him already looking at me. His hair had grown a little longer, but loose strands still fell over the right side of his face—an indication this was the real him. But I also knew it was him by the way he carried himself and how he ran his hand through his hair when in deep thought. *How did I miss this with that shadow creature?*

Osouf stood up from his seat, looking around the room. "I'm pretty sure sitting around and moping isn't going to get us anywhere. Let's go out and see what's going on, assess the damage."

"Give them some time to process," Ezrai said politely. His stubble was beginning to grey. "Although it is important to keep marching forward, it is just as important to rest."

"Excellent point," Alden chimed in. "Today's events may weigh heavy on us, and we don't know what to expect next. Whatever lies ahead, we should be well rested and strengthened. Take time to sharpen our swords, so to speak."

"Alright, then," said Osouf. "I'll check out Terah Region myself and observe the townspeople. If anyone would like to come, great. If not, suit yourself."

"Osouf, you more than any of us need to rest. Regain your strength." I glared at him. He shouldn't go out in his condition, having been held captive for over a month. Why was no one else concerned for him?

I looked to Ezrai, who only wore a neutral expression, and then the pack, who were still deep in thought.

"I'm alright," he assured me. "I've been resting long enough, cooped up indoors. Of course I'm ready to do something. Anything besides sitting here another minute." He moved to my side, and his hand rested on my shoulder. "If you're that worried, come with me."

Robin, who was leaning against the wall, came forward with a fierce expression. "I'll go." She folded her arms. "I need to check on some people."

My brother turned to me, waiting for a response. Truthfully, I too needed time to process everything. A sigh escaped me. "At least eat first," I suggested.

Kiran jumped in. "I made sure he had more food when I was forced to go back to the Alcazar. He looks better than he did."

I looked away from him. I searched the room for more volunteers, but there were none. "Fine. I'll go."

Osouf motioned for us to follow him out the door. Robin and I shuffled after him. The daunting orange sky waited for us outside.

The grim atmosphere was heavier than before. Many things remained unknown. How much power did Korland and the remaining avros have now? Would having one less crescent moon keep Ezrai from defeating Arah?

A shudder made my shoulders twitch. As if to add to the dark ambience, crows flooded Hyra, perching on rooftops and drinking from small, muddy puddles.

Shops seemed to be closed, but there were a few people outside, investigating the sky. Raven was one of them. Her arms were wrapped around her legs, her knees against her chest as she sat on the ground. Her body rocked back and forth. Something was off, but before I could mention it, Robin spotted her and rushed to her cousin's side.

Osouf and I followed closely behind. As Robin knelt beside Raven, I noticed the rocking didn't stop.

"Who is that?" Osouf asked me.

"Robin's cousin. She was once an avro, but Ezrai turned her back."

"Oh." He moved to crouch in front of Raven. Osouf met her gaze, which finally triggered a response. She stilled and then lunged back. Robin gave her arm a gentle pull, as if encouraging Raven to relax.

"It's okay. You're okay," she said.

"I-I…" Raven stuttered. Her pupils dilated for a moment. She cocked her head at my brother, raising a brow. "And who are you?" she groused.

"That's Osouf." Robin helped her cousin stand. Osouf kindly shook Raven's hand, but then his head whipped around, scanning our surroundings.

"We should get her inside her home." Osouf pointed at the house we stood beside. "Is this it?"

Robin shook her head. Raven's home was about four houses down. Though disoriented, Raven moved quickly, following our lead.

The moment we stepped inside his house, Finch ran to his daughter and enfolded her in a tight hug. He immediately let go and folded his arms.

"Girl, where have you been?" he questioned, both relief and frustration colliding in his tone.

"I don't know," Raven snapped.

Hearing the commotion, Falco stepped in. "Hey now, let's get situated, shall we?" Robin's dad ushered us to sit at the table while Raven disappeared, possibly heading for her room.

We all sat.

"It's imperative you keep an eye on her." Osouf gave Finch a stern look. "I hate to tell you this, but I'm seeing signs of her reverting back to avro."

Neither of the Jelani brothers appeared surprised, only somber as they leaned back in their chairs.

"Have you seen something like this before?" Robin asked, alarmed.

Osouf slowly exhaled. "Well, not exactly, but if Ezrai's power can restore avros, I'm sure in the wrong hands it can make them revert again. And, well…" His voice trailed off.

Falco made eye contact with Robin, who seemed to know just what her dad was about to ask. "I suppose that means no one knows how to keep it from happening, then?"

Finch was rubbing his face vigorously. I desperately wanted to tell him that everything would be okay, but how could I? There were thousands of Sairen wolves around Elohi, and only one king with the power to save us. And yet a piece of that very power was now in the hands of our enemies.

What good could possibly come from saving a few at the expense of his powers? Nothing…absolutely nothing.

I cleared my throat in an effort to keep tears from falling. A few escaped but were quickly wiped away before anyone noticed. All eyes were on Finch, who finally stood up and walked over to the window.

"How—" He paused, searching the outside world through the curtains. "How can I protect her?" Raven's father turned to face us with a desperate plea in his voice. "How do we stop this from happening, again?"

Osouf interlocked his fingers, his chin resting on them like he was praying. A lock of dark, wavy hair fell onto his forehead as he bent forward.

"I…don't know," he said reluctantly.

A loud clanging sound came from Raven's room, followed by a fierce wailing that we all knew belonged to Robin's cousin. Everyone rushed to Raven's room, crowding ourselves inside to a rage-filled Raven throwing things around the room. A dark-purple glow flickered in her eyes as Robin hugged her cousin.

"Please," Robin cried. "Not again. I'm not losing you again."

She wept, still keeping Raven restrained in her arms.

We all watched as the deranged young girl heaved, bending over with tears running down her cheeks. Finch knelt in front of his daughter, tears filling his eyes.

"You can fight this," he said. "I know you can, Raven."

Her head finally lifted. Somewhat calmer now, she pulled her shaking arm in front of Finch diagonally. With his arm, he met hers, making an 'X.' The Jelani family handshake.

Raven's father's lips quivered as he smiled, meeting her gesture with his right arm.

"That's right," he whispered. "Like the flock of birds."

A DEEP, SINISTER HOWL WOKE ME IN THE MIDDLE OF THE NIGHT. Alert, I sprang up in bed, eyes darting across the room before landing on the window as another monstrous howl rang through the night.

"What is that?" I asked aloud, though no one heard. Shariee continued to snore beside me. Nudging her softly didn't awaken her.

Whatever the creatures were, I discerned there were two of them.

Careful to not make a sound, I slid my legs out from beneath the covers and hopped smoothly to my feet. I tiptoed to the window, lifting one of the blinds to peek out. The sky was pitch black but tinged with red.

Having heard no thunder, and with barely a cloud in the sky, lightning startled me, but allowed me a quick glance at what lurked outside. Two enormous wolves stood amongst the trees.

They had no wings, but one seemed larger than Ezrai.

When another lightning strike lit up their faces, it seemed as though the smaller one had turned his head to glare right at me. I let go of the blinds, stepping backwards as I smothered a gasp.

I backed up into someone standing right behind me, which made my skin crawl. I swung around to see Cylus smirking.

"Somehow I knew I'd find you investigating." He did not attempt to whisper, though Shariee was stirring now.

"What is that supposed to mean?" I asked defensively.

He let out an irritated sigh and shook his head. "You know what I mean. I came in here because I too heard the howling and thought to myself, 'What kind of trouble will Lorraine get herself into now?' It didn't even occur to me that something dangerous was out there. No, instead I worried that *you* would go running after it."

"I wasn't going to," I said.

Cylus appeared miffed at my response. The narrowing of his eyes seemed to imply he thought that I was lying. A bit flustered, my hands fisted. But no words came to me.

Shariee rose from the bed, rubbing her eyes. She had slept with her hair in a ponytail. By now, the hair tie had fallen out and her golden locks formed a mane around her head. Confused, she glared at the two of us before muttering that she needed some water. We watched her leave the room.

My eyes strayed back to Cylus, who stood there with his arms folded. "I know it's hard for you to believe, but I promise, this time I had no thoughts of indulging my curiosity," I reassured him.

As I said it, I wondered whether it was the truth. Briefly, I had yearned to know just what creature was making that sound. What kind of threat would those wolves pose to the humans or us?

"I find that hard to believe."

"I know." The room grew cold, so I slipped back under the covers and curled into a fetal position, keeping an eye on the window. The whites of Cylus's eyes flashed as he too glanced out.

"Just stay out of trouble," he demanded. Peeking through the blinds, he added, "We stay low for now, unless otherwise directed by Ezrai himself."

"But isn't this the sort of thing we should be investigating?"

"Ezrai lost some of his power, so now is not the time to be reckless." Cylus rubbed his chin. "Perhaps we'll bring this to your brother."

"Where even is Ezrai?" I asked.

"He's meeting with some other packs of Sairens. I believe he is devising a plan with them before he comes back to us and lets us in on it."

As Cylus headed out of the room, Shariee came back with her glass of water.

"I've got to start drinking more water throughout the day. I always wake up parched." It was clear Shariee had no idea what was going on. She shrugged and crawled back into bed.

"Is anyone else awake?" I asked.

"Uh, other than Osouf and Robin, I don't think so."

I sat up, pulling my knees to my chest, pondering whether I should go check on her. She had been so worried about Raven. Although she annoyed me at times, I wouldn't wish family troubles on anyone. With an exasperated breath, my feet hit the floor.

Osouf sat on the couch, holding a hot cup of tea, while Robin stood in the kitchen. Cylus had joined them, too. I nearly twirled around to go right back down the hall but Osouf stopped me.

"Hey, you need something?"

I observed Robin and Osouf. My brother leaned back on the sofa with his legs about a shoulder-width apart, holding his mug with both hands. Robin stood on the opposite side of the room, partly facing Osouf, but her eyes were on her tea.

"Not really, I just thought…" I paused. Osouf glanced over at Robin and then stood up, finished his tea, and walked over to the kitchen.

"Whatever it is, just stay out of trouble, Lorraine." Osouf kept his gaze on me. I looked to Cylus, who just stood there leaning against the wall, snickering.

I rolled my eyes. The distrust I'd caused in everyone around me was understandable but agitating.

"Did neither of you hear those horrifying howls?" I asked Osouf and Robin.

"What—"

Cylus pressed his finger to his lips, prompting Osouf to listen closely. For a moment, there was nothing. Were they too far away now?

But then, off in the distance, a deep tune echoed. Osouf perked up, tilting his head as the sound faded.

"We should certainly bring this to Ezrai. Immediately," Osouf said.

Cylus and Osouf moved to the front door, while Robin finally looked at me. Her eyelids drooped. Stray hairs in her right eyebrow were standing straight up. Careful not to spill her still full mug, she placed it on the table in front of her and stepped forward.

Just before Osouf and Cylus made it out the door, it swung open and a panting Kiran stood there, catching his breath.

His eyes, two emerald jewels, scanned the room. One of Kiran's sleeves was folded behind his elbow while the other dangled loosely to his wrist. To my surprise, I noticed a dull glow behind him before he carefully shut the door. Could it already be morning?

"Where have you been?" Though my voice was dry, there was still an edge to my tone.

Osouf and Cylus moved away from the door. Cylus glared at Kiran. "Precisely what I would like to know. Where *have* you been?" He placed his elbow against the wall, cheek resting on his fist, like he was ready to be entertained.

Kiran ran his hand through his hair and blew out a breath. He sank into a chair. Without looking at anyone, he gestured in the direction of Hyra. "Just past Terah. There are monsters out there, as you know. That's where I've been."

"Don't toy with us; what were you doing?" Cylus demanded.

Suddenly, that feeling of familiar from before—back when Cylus revealed to me that he and Kiran had history—resurfaced. Maybe it was the resentment gleaming in those menacing silver eyes of Cylus's, or perhaps it was Kiran's consistent refusal to hold his gaze. Some sort of history lingered between the two of them, and a bad one at that.

Cylus's words echoed in my mind. "His ignorance cost the life of someone near and dear to me," he'd said. *Was it one of his parents? Both?*

"I was on official business, with Ezrai himself," Kiran explained, diverting my attention back to the present. "Arah retrieved his staff from Korland. He was here."

"Wait, *was?*" I blurted.

The bright-green eyes that had once sparkled at me were dull now. "Yes. Was. I imagine Arah is long gone by now. He disappeared into Hanska Forest. Ezrai says Arah cursed the forest so we couldn't chase after him." Kiran finally lifted his head. "And that's not all," he said reluctantly. "There were two…well…" As he seemed to struggle to search for the right words, it dawned on me just what he was trying to describe.

"The howling we heard. Two monstrous wolves?" I guessed.

"Something like that." He shrugged. "I remember a while back, my dad, um, Korland"—Kiran corrected himself—"was ordered by Arah to take Sairen wolf blood and mix it with an avro's. They had no idea what would come of it."

The two Sairen wolves that I'd seen in the Alcazar…were they the same as the two wolves we were hearing?

Robin's now empty mug slammed against the table in front of her. "We should be going after them." Her hand began to shake, so she pulled her arm back and held it still.

"No need to fret." Kiran glanced behind him at the door. "Ezrai has a plan." For the first time in a long while, he made eye contact with me. "He always does."

Unsatisfied, Robin bounced to her feet and marched straight up to Kiran. "Does this plan of his involve waiting till the very last minute? Till more lives are lost? How much more must we endure because he supposedly *has a plan*?" By now a handful of Kiran's black uniform was twisted in Robin's fist.

"Easy, Robin." Cylus clicked his tongue. "You're starting to sound like Lorraine."

Both of us simultaneously turned to look at him. Kiran's shirt was released now that Robin's fury was redirected at someone else.

Before anyone else could add to the tension clouding the cabin, Ezrai opened the door. Dasan stood beside him.

Robin returned to her seat.

There was something about Ezrai in his human form. He was nearly as powerful and magnificent as his Sairen wolf form. Those piercing dark eyes showed no sign of fear or worry. Although he stood on two legs, I saw his wonderful Sairen wolf form in my mind and was mesmerized. He carried himself with dignity. Though it was evident Ezrai and Dasan were here for a reason, the king grinned at us with genuine warmth.

Dasan's hands were shoved in his pockets, his thin lips pressed into a line. The uneven appearance of the grain in his leather jacket made my trainer seem tougher than usual. He carried his head high, like he was ready to pick a fight.

Ezrai scanned the room, his eyes landing on Cylus. "Wake everyone." Then, his smile vanishing, he said, "It's time."

Goosebumps covered my arms. I eyed Robin, whose eyes sparkled at Ezrai. Was that hope plastered on her face? Just moments ago, she'd been nearly strangling Kiran over his words of trust in Ezrai, but now she gawked at the king with excitement in her expression.

Exhausted as she must be, Robin jumped to her feet once again and then shuffled across the floor till she was standing directly in front of the king.

"Please," she whispered. "Please save my cousin. She's turning back." Tears trickled down her face. She didn't even bother to wipe them away; instead, she got down on her knees, holding Ezrai's hand against her forehead. "Raven is like a sister to me."

My heart tugged at her desperate tone; everything in me wanted to help. I felt the urge to run out the door, find Raven, and snap her out of her trance. I couldn't stop there, of course—all of them were calling out to me, the suffering souls that were drowning in the darkness. Especially the ones that painted my hands red—like the boy in the forest, and all of the lives I'd cost through my carelessness up to this point.

My chest felt heavy. Ezrai looked at me with concern, and then back down at the young woman kneeling in front of him.

The king cupped his hand around the back of her head and gently pulled her upright. "Stand."

I glanced over at Kiran, whose mind seemed to be elsewhere. It was difficult to look at him. All I could see was the shadow of a person I had once known.

"Of course I'll go," the king said.

I stood in awe. Shouldn't we be running after those monstrous wolves and stopping them? I wanted to help Raven too, but there wasn't time.

Robin wrapped her arms around Ezrai and squeezed. "Thank you!" she said gleefully.

"No disrespect intended," I said to Ezrai, "but after what happened at the Alcazar…your powers…"

Dasan took a step forward. "She has a point. How much was drained from you? Is this menial task something you should be doing?"

By now, everyone else had joined us. Some rubbed their eyes, still waking up, and others—mainly Luke—were eagerly waiting for an explanation.

Ezrai, smiling, studied each of us in turn. "Not to fret, my good friend," he said to Dasan. "I have hidden powers our enemy does not know about."

Jaws dropped across the room. Ezrai's expression turned grave. His brows furrowed, wrinkling his forehead.

It grew so quiet, I could hear insects singing outside the cabin.

"Although," Ezrai continued, "without the Ruach, I'll need time in-between to regenerate."

Arms folded, Osouf took a step forward. "Alright, so what's the plan?"

"First thing is tending to Robin's cousin," Ezrai stated, rubbing his hand over his short, scruffy beard. "Then we head to Hanska Forest, where Dasan and I spotted Arah." He glanced around the room. "Do not worry. We will be following behind Arah and Dasan will keep an eye on him up ahead."

"To do what, exactly?" Luke inquired.

Ezrai turned to him. "We can't meet him head-on right now. We will have to take care of other business first."

"I take it, those menacing howls we heard earlier?" Cylus watched the king carefully.

"Precisely," Ezrai said. "Besides, Arah will be building his army along the way…" He paused. "But so will we. If all goes according to plan, I have several more packs taking an alternate route, they'll meet with us in time."

"You mean we're headed for war?" Osouf asked, picking at his bottom lip.

"It's a very real possibility. Still, our goal for now is to remove Arah's main protection and then take back the stone. He's headed for Clarum Tower, which is a long journey from here. Outside of Hanska Forest lies a vast stretch of green hills that becomes rocky terrain. Even running at full speed, it would take Arah eight days to reach the Clarum Region. That's where he built his tower years ago, in preparation for if the Sairen wolf king really came as prophesized."

Outside of Hanska Forest…

I couldn't imagine it. Though I'd caught glimpses of the vast area opposite the cliffs, that was the most I had seen of a region other than Terah. What lay beyond the dense red oaks of Hanska had always been a mystery to me.

"We're following him there," Ezrai added.

"What's the deal with the tower?" Luke asked.

The king leaned down, eyes forward, his voice pitching lower. "From such a high tower, Arah can reach a multitude of land, covering a vast part of the world in his darkness and turning people into avros. Just like that." He snapped his fingers.

"And why hasn't he just done this before?" Shariee asked.

"Arah has had a hundred years to craft and grow his powers. It took some time to strengthen that staff of his but with the Ruach in its grasp and with the blood of one born under a red moon, he has a great source to draw power from."

RAVEN SLOUCHED AT THE FOOT OF HER BED. THE MOMENT SHE laid eyes on Ezrai, she hissed, squealed like a pig, and backed deeper onto her bed.

Robin reached out to her cousin with an unsteady hand. "It's okay," she whispered. "He's here to help you."

Raven's eyes darted to Robin, then rolled.

I was so exhausted that nothing really alarmed me. But I stood there, curious about Ezrai's power and how he'd heal Raven. Like the other Sairens, I was drawn to him.

Dasan stood beside the king, keeping anyone from getting too close. We all remained in human form, including Ezrai. The king cupped the troubled young woman's face in his hands and closed his eyes.

A strange warmth spread throughout my body as his power transferred to Raven. The clouds in her eyes vanished, a new light shining through them. Heat radiated from Ezrai. So many of us were standing in such a small space that I thought I'd break into a sweat at any moment.

Raven's eyes flickered, then filled with delight. Tears dripped down her cheeks as she gaped at the mysterious man standing in front of her.

Finch, Falco, and Robin threw their arms around Raven simultaneously. Her voice deep, yet a little unsteady, Robin said to Ezrai, "Thank you."

Needing some cool air, I slipped out of Raven's room, taking a deep breath. Dasan followed me to the living room. Was it too warm for him as well?

"Feel better knowing he does have some of his powers still?" he asked.

"Not really." I shrugged, keeping my eyes on the floor. "Do you?"

"I simply trust him." Dasan took a seat. "He's my closest friend. Not to mention, he's brilliant."

"Brilliant?" I scoffed, then snorted. "The most powerful Sairen wolf in the universe knowingly gave up a great amount of his powers because of my foolish ambitions. Tell me how that's so *brilliant?*"

The trainer chuckled to himself, playing with his mustache. "You still don't know, do you?"

"Know what?"

"He knew…" He paused. "That you would eventually sneak off to rescue your brother." His grin widened. "It's exactly what we were waiting for. All a part of the plan." Dasan released his facial hair and glanced up at me with an expression of amusement.

"What?" I said, collapsing into the chair behind me. My heart raced as I struggled to comprehend Dasan's statement.

"No need to be so ornery. Not everyone knew," he teased. "We knew Shariee would tell you; she can't keep secrets from you. Of course, Luke can't control himself. Kiran, Ezrai knew was not himself. Oh, and Robin. Ezrai insisted we didn't tell her, and for good reason."

"First of all, how do you know so much about us? You only came into our lives a few days…almost a week ago." I tried to keep my cool. My heart rate slowed, allowing me to think more clearly. "Why the secrecy?"

"Are you aware that those smoky wolf creatures can get into your mind the same way an avro can with a human?"

"You mean the Shadow Sairens."

"Yes. Point is, we didn't want them to know Ezrai was nearby, following you." Dasan smirked.

"But—" I was cut off by the door to Raven's room opening and everyone filing into the den.

Finch kept by his daughter's side. Raven, however, walked confidently, head high. She seemed different, even more different than the previous time she'd been returned to human form. Still, a fierce glare remained in her eyes as she walked towards us.

It occurred to me that someone with her determination and ferocity would make a great Sairen wolf.

"Will she be joining us?" I asked no one in particular.

"Nope," Raven was quick to respond.

After everything, she still couldn't trust us?

Falco seemed to notice the distasteful twist of my lips. "We would all love to follow Robin on this adventure. I'd go to war for my family, but sometimes not all battles are on the frontlines. Staying here to protect our little town is just as important as going after Arah."

"Right," Finch added as he slapped his brother's shoulder.

Ezrai nodded. With that, we said our goodbyes and returned to the cabin.

Just outside of the cabin, sitting by the lake, was Kiran. I waited for the others to go inside before I approached him.

"You are still you, right?" I joked.

His knees tucked into his chest and his eyes never straying from the water, he replied, "Yes, it's me."

I sat beside him. "Then why are you still so distant?"

Ignoring my question, Kiran laid down on his back, placing his arms behind his head like a pillow. "Korland will never change, will he? You think that's even possible?"

I took in a deep breath. "You mean your father."

He kept quiet.

"Well, he was human once," I suggested uncertainly. "What made him turn?"

Kiran turned his back to me. "Arah's darkness comes with many enticing features. Dad wanted to save mom, because she was ill and dying, but then she eventually passed and then he wanted to bring her back. He thought if he could gain power…but that power became an addiction. At some point, I think he forgot all about her." Kiran sat up. His shoulders moved back and forth as he drew in the sand.

"How could turning into one of those awful creatures bring back your mom?"

"Arah said with the Ruach and Ezrai's power, he could heal her. In order to steal Ezrai's power, Korland needed to become one of them…an avro." His arm stopped moving and he flipped over to his other side, this time facing me. "Like Dad, I wanted to save her, and for a while, I was a part of that plan."

Blood began to boil in my veins. I'd been conflicted when I learned Korland was Kiran's father, but everything in me still wanted to believe Kiran had nothing to do with luring me into danger, whether that was through Ezrai's plan or Korland's.

I couldn't look at him. "That's why you just showed up, not knowing a single one of us. You weren't there to help us save Osouf, you were there to help your father lure me into a trap." My eyes shifted to his hands, which repeatedly contracted and relaxed.

"It's not that simple," he said. "I really did want to help you. You see, when Ezrai found me, he gave me a choice and I chose to be freed from the darkness. The plan was tricky. First, I went to my father in human form and told him I met the king. Osouf and I had become friends in the prison, so I bargained...let Osouf go and I'd bring Ezrai to him. I figured he wouldn't agree, and it was never my intention to actually lead Ezrai to him. He wanted me to bring the king to him before letting Osouf go, but when I left, I fully intended to find you and the others, and go rescue your brother. He eventually figured it out and set up the plan to use a reflected version of me instead. It was a foolish plan. I think deep down he knew that. And by the way, I'm not a complete stranger; Cylus and I go way back." With a deep sigh, he stood.

"How far back?"

"Far enough."

My teeth clenched so tight, I thought they'd break. Hands forming fists at my side, I kicked the sand and let out a frustrated scream.

"I am so sick of the both of you. You and Cylus." I stood, glaring at him. "What happened? What did you do?" It annoyed me, but suddenly I felt protective of Cylus. I knew the pain of losing someone close to me.

Kiran stared at me, nostrils flaring. "I'm the reason his sister is dead. Happy?"

My heart sank. Cylus had a sister? I pried some more. "How?"

A bit calmer now, Kiran looked away and then up to the sky.

"My father infiltrated my mind with his avro powers and turned me." He paused, swallowing. "It was my job to bring Sairens born under a blood moon to my father. But...even as an avro, I struggled to complete my task. I was much like Evan: somewhere between human and monster. I fought it...I tried. Luah was the first child I was tasked to bring to my father. She was supposed to be the first of many. Arah wanted me to be a gatherer for him, but I resisted."

"So then what happened to Luah?" I questioned coldly.

"Korland followed me, to observe. I didn't want to take Luah—I couldn't, but when I lingered on the thought that my mother could be saved, something flipped inside me. I felt compelled to complete the task." Kiran's eyes widened in terror. "Cylus came up behind his sister, and we made eye contact. That was moments before I turned into a monster. He had saved me a year before that from an avro. I whispered to him to trust me, not to move, because I figured my father would kill him. But of course, Cylus leaped at my father, who in return, held him down with the staff."

Kiran's brows furrowed. "I snatched Luah. I actually had no idea what my plan was, but I was going to figure it out. I never did, Lorraine."

I frowned at him.

"I brought her to Dad's prison, the Alcazar. He promised me that if we did what Arah asked, we could see Mom again. She died as we waited for Arah to heal her. And then, Arah promised he could bring her back to life, with Ezrai's power, not that I really believed him. I thought of ways to release Luah, to bring her back to Cylus before Arah arrived… It just never happened. And then Arah came and took her life."

My eyes strayed from his. I couldn't look at him anymore. This was the secret he'd been keeping from me all this time. *How? How could I trust him after finding out all of this?*

My temples pounded. I rubbed them in circles. Kiran's reflected version flashed in my mind—how easy it was to sneak into the prison. It was all part of Korland's plan. If Kiran had evil intentions, he wouldn't be able to take Sairen form—the reason the fake Kiran couldn't. *This is the real Kiran, and though he's troubled, he's good.*

WHEN I RETURNED TO THE CABIN, EVERYONE STOOD IN THE DEN. Once I appeared, all eyes shifted to the king, with a few standing from their seats.

"That's it, then," Dasan announced, unfolding his arms and glancing over at Ezrai. "Time for takeoff."

Ezrai gave a confirming nod. To my surprise, even Luke was silent. Cylus bent down to grab a large satchel and slung it over his shoulder. Osouf and Robin simultaneously lifted their backs from against the wall.

We all filed out the door one by one, except Alden. His hand gripped the doorknob as he stood in the doorway. Hunched over with a weary grin, he said, "I'll be here, guarding Terah."

My heart sank watching him stagger back into his home.

It wasn't long before Alden's cabin was hidden from sight. Massive redwood trees lined our view of Hanska Forest. A fog flooded the forest floor, a nasty grey color with a hint of indigo.

"I'll race ya!" Luke elbowed Cylus. Though smiling, Cylus rolled his eyes while shaking his head. "Oh, come on. Shariee?" The young boy searched the group, hopping over to his sister.

"Not now, buddy, this is serious. Stop fooling around," she said lightly.

Luke pushed out his bottom lip and blew a lock of hair off his forehead. "Alright, fine." He hunched forward, hands in his pockets, kicking the ground as he walked. Shariee watched him from behind, her eyes never straying from the back of his head.

I turned to Ezrai. Surely he could see the ominous fog to either side of us. His eyebrows were drawn together, but he didn't slow. The king appeared melancholy, his forehead wrinkled. Still, he marched forward. His confidence both drew me and comforted me.

Ezrai strode ahead as we ventured deeper closer to the woods. He waved his hand in front of it. It seemed as though he used his powers to read the dark magic spilling from the trees.

"It's a quite specific curse," he announced.

Osouf lifted his head. "Specific how?"

Ezrai gazed around at the trees, as if he could see something we couldn't. "Ah." He paused, still examining. "Of course. Arah cursed the forest so that only one can enter."

"Well, that's annoying," Robin grumbled.

Cylus tilted his head at the king. "Can you not fix this?" He gestured to the forest. "Break the curse, or undo it?"

Hands behind his back, Dasan casually approached Ezrai. "It's not that simple, is it, dear friend?" Getting closer to the fog, he continued, "His Majesty could deplete any darkness, or curse, in this case, with the snap of his finger." He turned back around to face the king. "Perhaps this is no simple curse, there must be something tricky about it. Tell us then, what's the catch?"

"This curse has to be broken by facing your fears," Ezrai said.

Dasan's eyes widened as he rubbed his chin. "Ah. Clever, as I said."

"One of you want to enlighten the rest of us?" Robin inquired.

I popped my knuckles one by one. My mind felt clouded.

"The king fears nothing," Dasan answered. "Therefore, he cannot be the one to break the curse."

Ezrai gazed at the forest without moving a muscle.

"I get it," Osouf said. "Either Arah thought Ezrai wouldn't notice the details of the curse and would proceed ahead, trapping himself inside without a way to break it, or he simply hoped none of us could."

The king turned to my brother. "Perhaps Arah knows there's a possibility one of you could, but he hopes to delay us longer."

"Is the entire forest cursed?" Shariee asked.

"Yes, and skyward, so flying over is not optional." Ezrai responded.

"Alright, then," Dasan nearly shouted. "Who are we sending?"

"What about you?" Robin suggested.

Ezrai gave a firm "No" before the trainer could speak. He scanned the rest of us briefly.

Then it happened. The king and I locked eyes, sending a chill down my spine. The ground beneath my feet trembled as he spoke my name.

"Lorraine."

Murmurs broke out amongst my peers. The loudest protest came from Cylus, who didn't hold back. A vein bulged in his temple as he spoke. "You trust her out of all of us here to complete this task?"

His outburst made me feel dismayed. The urge to defend myself crept in; however, he had a point. My eyes watered.

Dasan took a step back, mouth gaping. His eyes darted to Ezrai, who remained unphased.

The king frowned at Cylus, tilting his head slightly. Maintaining his poise, he took a few steps closer. "And I suppose you're ready to face your fears?"

Cylus swallowed, clenching his jaw. He shifted to look at Kiran, giving him a menacing glare. "Of course not."

Kiran toed the dirt with his boot. I hoped he would look at me, let me read him, but he avoided my gaze entirely.

I observed the trees in front of us. Up close, they were daunting. "Ezrai, I can't even Spark. How—"

"Special powers are not needed for what you will face," the king stated as he placed his hand on my shoulder. A warmth ran over me, stilling my twitching muscles. "I'll be with you in spirit."

I breathed in deeply, then exhaled slowly.

I had no idea what I would face in there, but I had no choice. Ezrai had chosen me. I repeated that to myself as I walked to the edge of the fog.

"Lorraine." I stilled. *That voice…*

I turned around, giving the king a peculiar stare. The realization struck me, it was Ezrai's voice speaking to me all this time. *But how?*

"Remember," he said, but his lips weren't moving. Still, I knew it was him. His gaze gestured at the forest. "Fear is the greatest enemy."

My heart pounded, each breath sending a sharp pain across my chest. A bit stunned, my eyes swept over everyone else. *Could they hear him too?*

But their expressions wouldn't come into focus, all I could see were blurred faces. What was happening to me?

A vague, purple film seemed to be separating me from the pack. I focused on it until the image was clear…I was already within the cursed wall. Already trapped inside; there was no turning back now. Why hadn't I argued? It would have been easy to refuse, to request someone else take on the task, but that no longer mattered.

I was here now.

My tongue stuck to the roof of my mouth. I glanced to my left and then right, waiting for whatever illusions the dark magic would conjure up.

For what felt like half an hour, I wandered aimlessly. It was just an empty, dark forest. My throat felt parched. Water seemed to be absent, at least in this part of the forest. My human legs grew tired from walking. I found a hollow log lying in the grass and decided to rest against it.

My eyelids began to droop as I leaned further into the dead tree. The air was strangely thick. A tiny spot of blood spilled from my cracked lips. "No sleeping till I find water," I told myself, forcing my body to sit up straight before I stumbled to my feet.

I listened for water. Wind whistled in my ears, but I could hear nothing more. The whistling grew louder until it became a tune.

I whipped my head around to find Mom humming an upbeat song as she plucked a dewberry from a bush.

"Mom?" I blurted, then remembered where I was. "No. You're not real."

"Lorraine." She sighed her disappointment. She cocked her head to the side and glared at me, and my heart leaped into my throat. "How could you?" Her words slid into me like a dagger. "It's your fault." The sadness in her voice dissolved and her eyes pointed accusingly at me. "It's all your fault."

I nearly choked on the small amount of saliva I could manage to swallow. "No, you're not real." My voice cracked as my eyes became blurry and wet. I shook my head, trying to avoid eye contact.

"Lorraine," another voice called out. Slowly, I lifted my eyes to find Evan. "It's all your fault," he repeated. "I'm dead because of you."

"No," I cried aloud. "You're not real. You're not really here."

Then came another. "Lorraine." The small boy that had been killed by the avro with the scarred wing stood in front of me. "It's all your fault."

"Stop!" I yelled at the top of my lungs. But it was no use; more voices called out my name, listing my failures.

"I mean, really." Robin's illusion stood in front of me. "The pack doesn't need you; you can't even Spark. I should take your place, don't you think?" She giggled as she shot an invisible arrow right at my heart. Though I knew it was fake, I flinched anyway.

Every voice remained, intensifying. They taunted me, and there was no way to shut them up. I ran my fingers through my hair and pulled till a high-pitched command burst from me.

"Stop!"

And finally, they did. Each ghost disappeared, and the woods grew silent once again.

I curled into a ball in the grass as tears ran down my cheeks. Why Ezrai had chosen me was a mystery. Too many mistakes followed me, each one more haunting than the last. Could it be that facing those I'd failed was what I feared? It must be true, because the thought of hearing their voices again was more than I could bear.

A grey object appeared in the distance, sticking out of the ground. Whatever it was, I couldn't bring myself to find out. Several times, I told my body to get up, but my muscles rebelled. My body felt numb.

The entire pack, including Ezrai, waited for me to break down the barrier that kept them from their path to saving the world. Yet, I felt nothing. The desolate forest became comforting; peaceful, even.

My eyes shifted to my hands. Though I couldn't command them to move, my fingers twitched ever so slightly.

I remained focused on them until the grey object from before suddenly appeared in front of me. There was no avoiding it this time. I glanced up to find a tombstone with bold, black letters that read:

Here lies Orlin Sapphire

But then the words lit up. Seeing that for the first time, whether it was bogus or not, made my father's absence all the more real. "Dad," I whispered. "I wish you were here."

I wept by his grave until my eyes were puffy. "I'd do anything to go back in time. I'd be a better daughter. Make you proud." After wiping my nose, I leaned over and hugged the tombstone. To my surprise, it was hard and sturdy, as if it were really here.

I waited to hear his voice, like the rest of them. But alas, the woods were silent. That was what made this trickery all the more daunting: the hope that my father might still be alive. But I'd seen his grave with my own two eyes. I just couldn't accept his death.

"Loss is a terrible thing, isn't it?"

My heart fluttered as Kiran folded his arms and leaned against a tree.

"What are you doing here?" I said, standing.

He gave a lopsided grin, stepping closer. "I'm not really here, remember?" Once we were face to face, he unfolded his arms, cupped his left hand under my chin, and stared into my eyes. "Though a figment of your imagination, I'm here to help you."

"Why you?" I asked, pulling my head back.

He shrugged. "You chose me."

Heat rushed to my cheeks. Kiran let go of my face and grabbed my clammy hand instead.

"No," I said. "If I wanted anyone here to help me, you'd be last on the list. Even Cylus would be here before you." I jerked my hand from his and took a step back.

"If that were true, perhaps Cylus would be the one talking to you right now."

Flustered, I worked up the courage to look him in the eye. "You're not here to help. This place is cursed, so what is it that I fear with you?"

"Lorraine," he said softly, moving closer. "You can't face that fear without first facing your feelings."

A pulsating beat drummed through my sternum and into my neck as his lips drew closer to mine. Stunned, I couldn't move, until his face morphed into Korland's. I slammed my hands into his chest, but he quickly turned into a cloud of dust. Reappearing as Kiran, he shook his head at me disapprovingly.

"You're wrong!" I yelled, marching up to him with clenched fists. "I know I've made mistakes. I've been clumsy and selfish. That's why I'm being haunted by all the voices of those who have died on my account." Tears welled once again. "So go away," I demanded.

Surprisingly, he did.

I shook uncontrollably, my knees wobbling as I stood there alone. A part of me wanted him to come back, but the emptiness of the forest was also comforting. Rain suddenly poured down, but I didn't care. I sank to the ground. In a fetal position, I lay there, welcoming the deluge till my clothes and hair were soaked.

It wasn't long before the voices returned, flooding my throbbing head. I attempted to shut them out by covering my ears, but it was pointless.

Ezrai…he said he was with me, but where? How?

I hollered in frustration, my screams echoing back at me. "I can't. You hear me, Ezrai?" I shouted. "I can't do this. You chose the wrong person."

I punched the muddied ground and closed my eyes. When I opened them, a ring of fire surrounded me.

"What…is this?"

Perhaps it was another deception. It was difficult to distinguish its legitimacy, because although I could feel the fire's heat, the other scenarios had also tricked my senses.

The fire diminished, and the rain let up. I took a deep breath and turned, looking up at the top of the trees.

"As painful as it might be, are you going to let all those deaths be in vain?"

Kiran came back, this time playing the role of the voice of reason. The other voices vanished as we made eye contact.

I straightened. "Of course not," I mumbled. "Or at least, that's not what I want." Knees tucked into my chest, I hugged my legs and rested my head over them. "How can I face them, though? How can I face any of this? Though the people are illusions, the circumstances are real."

I glanced up at Kiran. A longer strand of hair fell over his brow. He was no longer smiling. Instead, his eyes searched mine.

"They aren't exactly what you're afraid of, are they?"

My mouth gaped.

"It's you," he stated, just before vaporizing into dust.

"Kiran, wait—" I reached out for him, but froze at what appeared in front of me.

My stomach dropped, causing my heart to skip a beat. As I gazed at the rectangular object in front of me, I became paralyzed. Staring back at me from the mirror was…well, me.

34

I SQUEEZED MY EYES SHUT, FORCING MYSELF TO ONLY THINK positive thoughts. "I am a white wolf, capable of Sparking, as fearless as they come. I'm not afraid of you."

When I opened my eyes, though, I was still standing on two legs. My Sairen wolf form stood in front of me.

In a matter of seconds, the strong, fearless version of myself was gone. The human part of me appeared in my reflection, but she was ugly. Black, charcoal-like smears underlined her eyes, but the worst part was the pain in her expression. One arm dangled, the other holding it. Seeing this side of me sent a shiver down my spine.

I turned away, trying to catch my breath. Sweat trickled down my neck. The image remained. I refocused on the silver-framed vision.

She no longer seemed sad. A scream bellowed from deep within her. Terrified, my immediate reaction was to look away

212

once more.

"What's the matter, can't face the truth?" she teased. "You're a coward. Not a true white wolf. You're powerless. Clumsy. You…are…nothing."

"Lies," I mumbled feebly.

Regardless, doubts blossomed. I was doing my best to convince myself, but how could I? The woman in the mirror was me, after all—my reflection. Her words were my own thoughts, the darkest parts of me that I buried deep below the surface.

"How could anyone love you? You're so pathetic."

My heart started racing. How could I shut her up? Something stirred inside of me.

"You'll never make it out of here. You will fail them, again. Only this time, you'll also be failing all of humanity. Pity." She smiled at me. "You'll die here."

Then it clicked in my brain. *Die.* That was my only other option. I'd either die here, living for quite some time with misery as my only company, or I'd live.

The others depended on my survival.

"You'll die here," she repeated.

I reached into the mirror, the glass around my arm becoming a liquid goo as I grabbed my reflected self and pulled her out. There was no reason for me to believe that I could do such a thing, or that it was necessary. I merely acted on a moment of rage. Now, standing in front of me, she no longer seemed confident; rather, terror filled her eyes.

What now? When I'd pulled her out, I'd felt angry, and had every intention of fighting her. I wanted to destroy that part of me. But now, I pitied her.

She straightened, then fled.

"Wait!" On all fours, I raced after her. It must have been because it was simply an illusion, but she easily outran me.

Finally, she stopped, appearing and disappearing in different places around me.

Then she was in front of me. My mouth opened, but I couldn't find the words.

"Have something to say?" she asked.

This side of me was psychotic. Toying with me one minute, then drooping with sadness the next.

Another revelation came to me. She *was* me. The part of me that felt doomed to fail. The part of me that was reckless. The part of me that couldn't trust anyone. The part of me that I hated the most.

She was hurting. I could see that now.

"Yes," I began, mustering up my courage. "You're brave."

She was quick to disagree. "No, I'm not."

"Fierce," I said. "Strong-willed, although at times it has gotten you into trouble. But you are no mistake."

My voice cracked. The other me was beginning to fade.

"But you've made many mistakes," she countered.

"Out of everyone else out there waiting, Ezrai chose you." I felt my eyes widen. "He chose me." I pointed a shaky finger at her. "We can overcome, because something greater is at stake."

She shook her head. "You don't have the strength for that." Turning away from me, she corrected herself. "I…don't have the strength for that."

The pounding of my heart ceased, and the knots in my stomach released. I lifted my head, and before she completely faded away, I said, "You're right."

The mirror formed in front of me, along with my reflection staring curiously back at me.

"And that is why I must embrace this part of me, but shatter this image that I carry of myself. Ezrai gave me a purpose. I am valued by the king."

Imagining a crystal sphere in my hand made it so. The sphere glowed a bright, pure red.

Without hesitation, I threw the orb at the mirror. The silver surface shattered into tiny pieces till the mirror was no more.

A purple glow burst outward from where the mirror had been and then raced through the trees, which rippled in the light's wake.

It was done. The curse had been lifted. The illusions would no longer torture me. The forest was quiet, except for the stream of water nearby.

Water!

I rushed to find it. I didn't bother to wait for the pack; instead, I knelt beside the stream, cupping cool water in my hands and slurping it down.

I let out a satisfied breath as I sat on the pebbled bank. My eyes were swollen, but they no longer burned. My tense muscles relaxed.

Soon, the sound of the pack's footsteps drew near, their voices ringing with excitement. The pack must have seen the wave of purple light that signaled my success and came to find me. I rested my eyes while I waited for them.

Though they were close, since Luke never stopped yakking, a different voice, one that sounded much closer, had me springing to my feet.

"Lorraine?"

There was no mistaking it.

"Dad?" I spun. "Where are you?"

He never answered. Nor did I hear any movements, aside from the pack as they approached.

"Hey. You did it!" Shariee cheered.

Still uncertain, I greeted them warmly.

"I suppose I owe you an apology," Cylus said through gritted teeth. He took in a deep breath and, to my surprise, smiled. "You did well. Sorry I did not believe in you."

Many other compliments followed from the others. Dasan

was the only one who didn't acknowledge my success.

"Victory has not yet been won," said the trainer. "This was only a small portion of what lies ahead. Let's get moving."

My packmates slapped me on the back and shoulder, then moved onward. When it was Ezrai's turn, he kept his hand on my shoulder for a moment.

"Well done," he congratulated me. "Now look ahead; there is still much work to be done. Though a bit hasty, Dasan is not wrong."

As Ezrai and the others marched ahead, I lingered for a moment, scanning the forest one last time.

"Dad, if you're out there, I will find you. I promise."

A VISION PLAYED OUT BEFORE ME.

The place felt…familiar. I lay on my side atop a soft plushy substance that looked like grass, though it didn't feel like grass. The day was bright, but the shade of the tree above me sheltered my eyes.

Light sparkled in my peripheral vision. I turned my head to get a better view.

I jumped to my feet in disbelief. This was no ordinary tree; it was made of glass and clear as crystal, except for the leaves—though also like glass—which were a deep, radiant green.

Although I was in awe of its beauty, I felt a flicker of familiarity. *I've been here before.*

Without warning, a hand grabbed my shoulder, turning me around. Before I could see who the hand belonged to, the image vanished. I was once again in the forest with the rest of the pack.

"You alright?" Osouf asked.

"Yeah," I said, dazed. "I'm fine."

A golden-orange hue filtered through the trees. My eyes still felt heavy, but my heart was light. Anticipating the journey ahead gave me the adrenaline I needed to keep going.

Picking up my pace, I maintained my speed alongside Osouf. We all dashed through the forest in our Sairen wolf forms—waiting for Ezrai to tell us when to stop. The redwood trees appeared endless as we followed him for several miles.

Luminous, blue-and-white flowers lit our path. *Moonflowers.* They weren't rare on Elohi, but they didn't glow for long, blooming in the last week of summer and dying within the first few weeks of fall.

Though the flowers were beautiful, we continued to race through the forest. My heart swelled as thousands of moonflowers continued to light the way. My eyes didn't stray from them until I crashed into Shariee, who was stopped dead in her tracks.

"Hey—"

No one dared to move a muscle as a large black avro approached. A tremble began in my legs as the creature drew closer, staff in hand. Korland stood beside him.

My eyes immediately went to the Ruach. It was darker now; only a faint red shone, while some parts were orange. A black cloud swirled inside.

"Arah," Ezrai acknowledged the large avro, breaking my trance.

Hesitantly, I looked at Arah once more. Now that he was closer, I could see the violet tint to his leathery skin.

"Ezrai." Arah drove the staff holding the stone into the ground in front of him. "You know, *king,* it's occurred to me that Kor here has failed to extract all of your powers." He dipped his head, giving Ezrai a menacing stare.

My legs wobbled beneath me. *Stop it. Get a hold of yourself.*

With a deep inhale, I began to gain more control over my

body.

Ezrai took a step closer.

"I'd tread carefully if I were you." Arah positioned himself behind Korland, the two monstrous wolves appeared beside him. Like the shadow Sairens, they had red eyes, but they were no shadows. One was black and almost just as large as Ezrai. The other white and closer to the average Sairen size. "You're lucky I can't just kill you to get what I want. Ugh, you're so complicated. But I've figured out your little secret." The hideous monster taunted as he circled Korland, who tightened his jaw, glaring at Arah.

Ezrai took another step, and then paused as Arah continued to talk.

"Seeing that faded crescent moon of yours proves my theory."

A growl escaped King Ezrai.

"Still think I don't know?" Arah sniggered. "Your power comes in three parts. Which is precisely why I have a three-part plan. Phase one…" Now standing behind Korland, Arah pushed him forward. "Manipulate Kor here to take care of power piece number one, one crescent moon down. Only two left…which brings me to phase two."

My heart skipped a beat. I lifted my paw to move forward, then froze. Arah hovered his hand over Korland, a black cloud-like power flowed from his hand. It looked as though life was being sucked out of Korland. *Arah really has powers of his own?*

Korland paled, but remained an avro. Kiran's father coughed and let out a cry, then fell to the ground. Several gasps filled my ears.

"We—" he whined. "We had a deal." He coughed again, this time wheezing.

"Dad!" Kiran ran to his father, kneeling beside him. It startled me at first, seeing Kiran cry over the one who'd caused him so much heartache. The one who caused *me* so much heartache.

But it's his father.

I couldn't bear to watch them, so I looked to Ezrai instead.

"Time is ticking," Arah said.

The king took one last step before transforming to human and running over to Korland. He placed his hand on Kiran's shoulder, saying something inaudible to him.

Still beside Korland in the grass, Ezrai glared up at Arah. "Someday, Arah, I will take back what belongs to me, and you *will* reap what you sow." Ezrai placed his hand on Kiran's father, quick to get a bit of his power through him before it was absorbed by Arah's staff.

Arah jerked the staff back to his side, and Ezrai stood firm. Something wasn't right, Arah seemed to pull the staff forcefully, as if the Ruach pushed back. But he still straightened with a gloating expression.

Arah glanced around at our terrified faces and snickered. He used the staff to keep us in place.

Ezrai closed his eyes momentarily. *What was he—*

"Ready yourself." That voice...the low whisper of the Ruach. It was speaking to Ezrai. *Can anyone else hear it?*

"Soon," Ezrai said. But his lips didn't move. He quickly transformed to Sairen wolf and glared at the wretched monster.

Arah approached the king and lifted Ezrai's chin with his claw, bringing them face to face. "There it is—only one bright crescent moon remains. Phase three is already in action. We'll see each other again soon." Retracting his claw, Arah straightened, now meeting our glares. "Sairen wolves, I present to you, your king," he mocked.

Cackling, Arah turned around and disappeared into the forest.

Keep reading for a bonus chapter from Ella's perspective…

Bonus Chapter

Ella

A SMALL RAY OF SUNSHINE PEERED AT ME THROUGH A CRACK IN THE WALL. I grinned at the light and chipped at the wall beside me. It had been three days since I was escorted to Arah's personal prison. Three days of being stuck in nearly complete darkness. The cell was empty and there was no one to talk to.

At least in Korland's prison, there was plenty of commotion, and there was Jae—the girl I'd become good friends with. We made up songs together and harmonized inside the prison. We kept score over who could sing the loudest and get Korland or one of his guards to come shut us up. Jae was always the loudest. Her voice boomed down the halls like no other I'd ever heard before. My own voice was too soft.

At times, we'd had enough fun that we would forget we were stuck in a prison. Of course, that thought wouldn't last long. Jae longed for her parents and herself to be free—they were trapped there together. I wanted to be back home with Dad, who I know was going crazy trying to find me.

I imagined at times, what Dad was doing, what he was thinking, but it only hurt me more, because I knew he was gravely troubled by my kidnapping. That night had haunted me each passing day since I was taken.

A villager had requested my help with his mare, who had broken her leg. Dad told me not to waste my time and healing powers on an animal, but it was important to the owner. His whole family loved that horse. I tended to her leg. The blue glow that surged through my hand reached inside the mare's body. The inflammation gave off enough heat that it made the break quick to find and with a curl of my fingers, brought her bone back together.

"Thank you, thank you so much!" The wife said, teary eyed. "May the Light bless you."

I gave her a warm grin, and twirled around in the direction of home. But, as I had turned to face the other direction, I caught glimpse of something...*someone. Am I being watched? Oh stop it Ella, you're being silly.*

I trudged on home, only to find that someone had beat me there...Korland.

With the staff in his hand, he forced my father to the ground.

"Please, no, what do you want?" I asked, my heart caught in my throat.

"You."

My Dad fought the force of the staff to simply shake his head "no" at me.

"First, tell me why," I demanded with a shaky voice.

"Arah has special plans for you," he said. His eyes shifted to my Dad. "For both of you."

No, not Arah.

"Ella, no. Whatever should happen to me, is certainly worth Arah not getting what he wants. Run now, get out of here."

I gazed into his eyes as Korland pushed further with the staff. My father cried out in pain.

"Please, stop," I shrieked. I turned away, but could still hear the painful groans. Tears flooded my eyes and rolled down my cheeks. *Dad is right. Arah can't have what he wants.*

I jolted forward and bent my knees, ready to run.

"Ahhhh," Dad shouted. I spun around to see the gut-wrenching pain in his eyes.

"Stop," I cried. "I'll go. Just leave him alone." Glancing over at Dad I whispered to him. "Sorry Daddy, I just couldn't let you die. We'll figure this out."

My memory faded as the door finally opened for the first time in three days. Sure, someone made certain to slide some grub under the door each passing day. It was just enough to survive. But now, the door had opened. Light flooded my surroundings. Still, a darkness invaded the atmosphere. It was Arah.

"Ah, there you are. Such a pleasure to finally meet you. Have you enjoyed your stay?" The evil creature grinned. With rapid breaths I tried to keep myself still, but my body trembled. I didn't know whether to actually respond or keep quiet and look away.

What does he want from me? My healing powers? No, I won't heal him.

My thoughts stilled when Arah moved in closer. "Cheer up, you get to see your precious Daddy today."

I perked my head at him. The shaking stopped but my heart continued to rapidly beat.

"What do you mean?" I asked. My words slurred together.

"Just a quick looksie," he teased. "Now, come with me." With a wobbly step forward, I began to follow. *Am I really going to see Dad? Or is Arah toying with me?*

Acknowledgements

First, I give thanks to God for his amazing grace and sovereignty. Reflection would not have made it this far without my helper, friend, and savior. Thank you Lord for guiding me and being with me through every step of the way. Even through my failures, you can do great and mighty things. A huge thank you to my husband, Noah, for your emotional support and hard work so that I can chase my dream. Who knows how many more years it would have taken me to publish without you. You have given me plenty of encouragement and provided snacks for those late nights of editing. You pushed me even when I felt like giving up. I love you and appreciate all you've done to get me here. To my daughter, Melody, you are the light of my world and I hope one day you will know that you are fearfully and wonderfully made. To my family: parents, siblings, grandparents, cousins, aunts and uncles. To all of my in-laws. All of you have a part in my life that has shaped me to be who I am today and therefore you all have a part in this, so thank you. Shout out to my bestie and sister-in-law, Min, who encouraged me in the early stages of my publishing dream, and helping me with the story development. Thank you. Monica, my dear friend, thank you for your excitement for *Reflection* and for all the writing days in the past and many more to come. You helped fix some of those pesky plot holes by lending me your ear and helping me bounce off ideas. And don't worry Michael, I didn't forget you. You are Monica's other half, so when I say "Monica" I mean you too. Lastly but very importantly, I thank my 4th grade teacher, Mrs. Henderson who said I'd become an author one day. Your words and enthusiasm have stuck with me. I'm so glad I get to prove you right!

About the Author

Crystal has been writing stories since she was nine years old. She's always been a big daydreamer, keeping her from being able to focus on other work. Born and raised in Texas, Crystal loves a variety of foods. Indian and Korean bbq are some of her favorites. Publishing has been her dream since elementary school. When Crystal isn't writing, she enjoys spending time with her family and church family, reading, playing video games, watching Star Wars with her husband, and fishkeeping.